STAKING HIS CLAIM

MEN IN CHARGE
BOOK 2

TORY BAKER

Cover Design by LJ with Mayhem Cover Creations

Photographer by Emina with TGTRN

Models: Luke Matthews & Lizzy Hofweber

Editor Julia Good with Diamond in the Rough Editing

❋ Created with Vellum

Tough times never last, but tough people do.
Unknown

PLAYLIST

Staking His Claim Playlist

From the Start- Matt Schuster
Van Gogh- Pony Bradshaw
This Damn Town- Arlo McKinley
The Kind of Love We Make- Luke Combs
Whiskey On You- Nate Smith
Last Night- Morgan Wallen
Motorcycle Drive by- Zach Bryan
Memory to Drown- Bryan Martin
Cardigan- Taylor Swift
Champagne Supernova- Oasis
Thinkin' Bout Me- Morgan Wallen
The Freshmen- The Verve Pipe
Here Without You- Three Doors Down
Please Don't Go- Wyatt Flores
Oklahoma Smokeshow- Zach Bryan
If We Said Goodbye- Megan Moroney

Flower Shops- ERNEST & Morgan Wallen
Pretty Heart- Parker McCollum
Rock and a Hard Place- Bailey Zimmerman

BLURB

I want the one woman I should never touch.

Tulsa Rose has gone through hell and back.
We have a complicated history, becoming her guardian after
a family tragedy is only the tip of the iceberg.
I sent her away.
It was the right thing to do, even if she felt like I turned my
back on her.
The truth is, she was a temptation I couldn't have.
She was way too young.

Now she's home, ten years later.
I want her more now than I ever did.
Too bad she hates me.
It doesn't matter.
I'm not walking away from her again.
She belongs to me, she always has.
I'm staking my claim once and for all.

This is the second book in the Men in Charge series, each book will be a complete stand alone, the common denominator? An alpha Hero, a man that goes after what he wants, a guaranteed happily ever after, and of course steamy romance!

PROLOGUE

Ledger Sinclair, Age 27

I never thought I'd be in the position I am now. My best friend is gone, way too soon, and way too fucking young—Montgomery Williams. The same age as me. We were childhood friends. There'll be no more dinners, no more sitting on the front porch shooting the shit while enjoying a beer at the end of a long-as-hell day.

How the hell this could happen to a man as loyal as Mont, I've got not one damn clue. The call I received in the middle of the night jarred me awake. Nothing good comes from the phone ringing at two o'clock in the morning. The person on the other end of line, Tulsa Rose, seventeen years old, a girl turning into a woman, didn't speak a word. There are only three people on this earth who could have been calling me—Mont, Tulsa, or my mom. Considering there was a shit ton of sniffling coming from the other end of the line, I knew. My stomach sunk to my feet. Neither of us said a word. Feeling like I was about to be sick, I swung my legs over the edge of the bed, one hand holding my cell to my ear, my forearm on my thigh, trying to gain my composure before making my next move. What seemed like a lifetime later when in fact it was only fifteen minutes, I was dressed, out the door, and driving the few short minutes between my place and the Williams'. The two cop cars were parked behind Tulsa's car. Mont's truck wasn't in his usual place. The second I was out of my truck, long limbs were running toward me, tears streaking down her face, hair flying behind. All I could do was brace for impact as she leapt into my arms, feeling her tears saturate me as Tulsa let loose. It was only once she fell asleep in my arms after hours of sobbing while I sat on the front porch steps that Judd and his dad told me what happened. Judd, a friend of mine and Montgomery's, and his father, who'd been on the force for years, told me how it all went down. Mont was traveling home when he was t-boned by a drunk driver. Dead on impact. At that point, I was holding tighter to Tulsa than I probably should have, and it was me who had wetness coating my cheeks this time. It was less than a week ago that the news shattered our world.

Today is the funeral, and to say that things aren't going well would be putting it lightly. Tulsa has completely shut down—eyes downcast, body sunken in on itself, looking like she lost more weight than she can afford to lose. I can't say I blame the girl. The Williams family has not had it easy. Shit coming in threes fucking sucks, especially for the girl standing next to me.

"We're so sorry for your loss." Those words are repeated over and over again at the graveside service we're currently holding for Montgomery, his final resting space right beside his family in what is now a family plot in a cemetery here in our hometown.

"Thank you," I respond. Tulsa's body is leaning against mine. Her hand moves from its place on my bicep down to my fingers, entwining them with mine. My body twitches at the wrong fucking time. Montgomery knew that Tulsa had no problem prancing in front of me. So close to being eighteen yet not, she assumed the looks she gave me were one-sided. They absolutely were not. I had to talk myself out of so much as glancing in her direction when she would walk through the house in her bathing suit making way to the pool at their house. I curse myself at the feeling of her tits pressed against my arm. She's too young, gone through too damn much in her short life to be saddled with someone ten years older than her.

"Ledger." Tulsa squeezes my hand to get my attention.

"Yeah, Tulsa?" Her head tips up slightly as mine lowers.

"I need to get out of here. It's too much." Eyes that are usually a clear hazel color are now blood shot.

"Go ahead. I'll handle the rest of this. It shouldn't be too much longer." She wraps her arms around her frail body. I make a mental note that I'm going to have to make sure she takes care of herself.

"Thanks." She nods before she takes off, the black dress whipping around her body with the wind. You can smell the precipitation in the air, a sure sign of the rain that will likely start pouring down any moment now. Hopefully, this will be wrapped up, so we can head to the attorney's office. Tulsa can eat then finally get some damn sleep. And me, I can drown myself in a bottle. It doesn't matter what kind of bottle it is either—beer, tequila, vodka, whisky, or bourbon, all five would be good with me right about now. Anything to drown out the thoughts that Montgomery is gone, and I'm left with the memory of how Tulsa and her firm little body feels against mine.

PROLOGUE

Tulsa Rose, Age 17

If someone had told me I'd lose three of the most important people in my life within years of one another, I would have told them it's impossible. There's no way my mom would have passed away when I was only ten years old. A massive heart attack while Dad was at work, I was at school, and my brother was away at college. My father greeting me at school in the middle of the day should have been a warning. The turmoil was written all over his face, except I was young and didn't realize what was going on, so I ran toward him, a smile plastered on my face thinking he got off work early and was treating me to a day away from school with ice cream. That wasn't the case. He explained to me when he didn't hear from Mom at her usual check-in time around lunch, he had a weird feeling that something was wrong, so he went home, where he found her unresponsive. It was years later that I learned she had an undiagnosed heart condition, and the reason us kids had to have a cardiologist work up to make sure the gene didn't pass to Mont or myself. Two years after that, Dad passed away in his sleep, from a broken heart.

Montgomery, God, how I'm going to miss my big brother. He picked up the broken pieces of our life. He was already the brother; it was the father and friend roles that became wrapped up all in one. He held the remainder of our family together, and now I'm not going to ever get to have those talks over ice cream when a boy at school annoys me or when the time of the month hits, and the world feels like it's hitting me at every single angle. God, I could really use him right about now.

Instead, I'm sitting in an attorney's office in town with Mr. Flay. Ledger is sitting beside me as we hear the final words of Montgomery's last will and testament.

"Tulsa, Ledger, hate like hell that I'm once again here with your family," Mr. Flay says, looking at me.

"Yeah, I can't say that I blame you," Ledger replies. I've been quiet, lost in my own thoughts, worrying about everything that's going to happen from here on out, how I'm going to get through a single day. I'll be honest—contemplating it is a struggle.

"Ledger, you've been given guardianship over Tulsa Rose. Montgomery wants her to go to school in Alabama, the school she chose, and she'll be doing it as soon as possible. There's been money set aside for daily expenses as well as on-campus living. Ledger will be responsible for taking care of the family home while Tulsa is away." I gasp, appalled. How could Montgomery send me away? It's bad enough everyone else in our family has left me, and now this. An imaginary knife twists deeper inside my heart.

"I'm not going to Alabama. I don't care what Montgomery says. I'll stay here and go to college." I stand up, feeling dizzy as I do, cussing myself black and blue because my appetite has been gone. Not even my favorite comfort foods are appealing.

"You're going to Alabama. You've been dreaming and working your whole damn life to get into that college. If this is what Mont wants, it's what you'll do." Ledger's voice is unlike I've ever heard it before—deeper, darker, angrier. That's good because the feeling is entirely mutual.

"It's a good thing you're not the boss of me, Ledger Sinclair," I mouth off, hands going to my hips, stomping my foot. I hate today. I hate all days. I hate Mondays, Wednesdays, and I especially hate Saturdays. But today, Tuesday, might give the rest of the days I lost my family a run for their money, today is the icing on the cake.

"I've got a piece of paper that says I am, so get over your little snit. Why would you want to stay in this small town? You're seven-freaking-teen. I'll keep the house the way it's been until you've graduated. Spread your wings, live your life to the fullest. Montgomery didn't get that chance. And don't start. He never once begrudged anyone for that, but he damn sure wanted to give you everything he could," Ledger says. I can't take it anymore. The world as I know it is no longer my own. I spin on my heels and run for the door, not ready to lose what little dignity I have left. I push the doors open with an energy I thought was long gone with my head staying down. The reception area is empty minus Leslie, Mr. Flay's secretary. Even she doesn't say a word. I'm pretty sure this isn't her first time seeing people run away from their problems because that's exactly what I'm doing. The next door gives just as easily. The fresh air, the hot sun, the slight breeze, it's what I need, and it's all about to be taken away from me. Yes, I'm aware Alabama still has the same air, sun, and weather as Florida, but it's not home. It's not Orange Blossom.

My ass hits the curb. The concrete is hot and feels good beneath my funeral dress as I wrap my arms around my knees, head tipping to the side. The tears I thought were coming are suddenly bone dry. "You didn't have to run away, Tulsa. We could have talked."

"Go away, Ledger," I mutter, opening my eyes to look at him, at his soft wavy brown hair, chiseled jaw, angular nose, green eyes, a full beard that's short and trim, and the same dark circles that match the ones I have beneath my own.

"Not happening. Come on, we've got some talking to do, butterfly," he calls me by a name I haven't heard him use in years, hand out and requesting me to take it in a quiet manner.

"I think it'd be better if talking weren't necessary." His calloused hand slips around mine, engulfing me in more ways than one. Ledger helps me off the ground and pulls me into his body, allowing me to rest my head on his chest, arms going around his waist. I should hate him. He's so readily willing to push me away, and what do I do? I burrow into him further, breathing in his presence, a mix of leather, pine, and bergamot, a scent I've known for as long as I can remember. Any chance I could get to be near him, I took full advantage of—a hug hello, a wave here and there. I soon figured out he wasn't as immune to me as I once thought he was.

"Spread your wings, Tulsa Rose, be the butterfly you were always meant to be. Come home for the summer if you want or stay up there; it's entirely up to you. But you've got to do this, even if you hate me for driving you away." He may be breaking my heart bit by bit, word by word, but I know one thing for certain: he's not as unaffected as he plays off to be.

My body is flush against his, a presence against my stomach. There's no way it could be anything else than Ledger's length. Hard, clearly thick, girthy, and long judging by the way it's jutting upwards. One day, I'm going to make Ledger Sinclair regret the day he pushed me away.

1

TULSA ROSE

Ten Years Later

It's a sad state of affairs when you have no one to come home to. True to his word, Ledger Sinclair took me to Alabama. The ink on the death certificate was barely dry before he was driving me away from the life I knew and loved. The anger, hurt, and betrayal lingered in my body the entire way. I guess the good news is that the will did state the money from the estate would keep up the house. Ledger would do check ins every other week and was asked to stay while the house was cleaned seeing as how all of my family's worldly possessions were locked away inside. I breathed a sigh of relief. That still didn't mean I spoke a word to him the entire drive up. While being accepted to the university I'd hoped and dreamed of early in my senior year of high school was amazing, what wasn't awesome was having zero family to celebrate it with. A huge accomplishment, but it

left me feeling empty inside. All of the extra classes to grad-
uate early seemed to have backfired. If I had stayed the
course like most teenagers, I could have stayed in Orange
Blossom. Instead, I was in Alabama for a minor in business
and major in interior design. I'm proud of what and who I
became for the most part, though I've still got a long way to
go in overcoming so much trauma as a child and young
adult. Thankfully, that's what therapy is for. Another reason
for why I'm just now making the trek back home, ten years
later instead of returning after I graduated college. You see,
there was a time when Ledger would answer my calls and
texts, until I called him after a particularly long session of
therapy, where I told him I hated him and wished it were
him instead of Montgomery who'd died in the crash. At least
someone would still be on this earth who loved me. The
absolute worst thing I could say and entirely my fault. When
I tried to get a hold of him two days later to apologize, the
text I sent first came back not delivered and the phone call I
placed said his phone line was disconnected. Another phone
call placed to Mr. Flay let me know that Ledger was still
around and taking care of what was asked of him, meaning
I'd really bungled up life. I did the next best thing after once
again talking to my therapist—writing a letter explaining
how sorry I was, along with a few other things. And what do
you know? It was returned to sender.

That was five years ago. I quit trying after the last ditch
effort was tossed out the window, another phone call to Mr.
Flay, making sure there was enough money in the estate to
maintain the upkeep of my family home. It was a no-brainer
—bury your head in the sand along with everything else,
take a job in Alabama, and go on with life. *Until now.*

"You can do this, Tulsa Rose. You didn't come all this way

to only come all this way," I say as I step out of my car and look at the house. Both inside and outside hold all of my happy memories along with a crap load of bad memories, amazing in the way that this is where Mont and I grew up, watching our parents dance in the kitchen, baking cookies after school, aggravating one another for no other reason than we were siblings. So many great times were built in the two-story home sitting on a few acres of land with a small pond in the back. Where I'm hoping to start fresh. Alabama was never the place I felt at home. Nope, I'm a Florida girl through and through. I close the door to my car and put one foot in front of the other, even though there's a tingle in my hands, a tightening in my chest, and the blinking of my eyes as I take my first step up the front porch. The guilt I feel for allowing Ledger to control when I came home hits me deep. Breathing becomes harder, and before I know it, I'm reaching for the railing, using it as leverage as I drop to my ass, close my eyes, and give myself a moment. The affirmations my therapist told me to use come to mind. I am strong, I am brave, I am loved, and I can do this. Yeah, that 'I am loved' part is hard to swallow. There's one person on this earth who does love, me and it's my best friend and now former roommate, Nelle. The love we have for one another is real. We pick each other up when the other is feeling down, celebrate the victories no matter how big or small.

"Nelle, I can't do this." The call is placed without my realization, so distraught at the idea of walking through the front door, not having my mother, father, or brother. Never mind Ledger, who lives right next door. I will never call him, not like I can or would. Though, I'm sure one call to Mr. Flay, and he'd give me Ledger's new number. That's no longer an option in my eyes.

"Tulsa Rose, you can do anything," she responds without the pleasantries. We don't need those, considering we spoke an hour or so ago, when I checked in with her, Nelle telling me how our apartment isn't the same without me there. I'm secretly hoping she'll move down here eventually.

"I'm not sure I can do anything. I barely made it to the last step on the front porch. What if I'm making a mistake?" On a whim, I applied for a job in a bigger city next to our town. The commute would mean twenty minutes each way, not too bad considering I wouldn't have to live in said city, where it's not near as peaceful as Orange Blossom.

"Well, you can always come back to Alabama. Your room is still empty, but, Tulsa, you may not be able to admit this to yourself, so I'll do it for you. The woman you are is not because of a house. It's who you are in your heart. Plus, would you really be able to admit defeat, come back with your tail tucked between your legs and give up your position as lead designer at Restore and Repair?"

"I hate when you're right. Do you realize how unfair that is?" Restore and Repair, easily known as R&R, is known for working on homes that have been restored to their former glory. My job there is an absolute utter dream come true. Whereas the other side of the firm buys homes, repairing or rebuilding homes from the 1800s to the 1970s, my side is sourcing everything from paint to wallpaper, light fixtures, bathtubs, and all the items you'd need to make it a true home it represents. There's something to be said about a house full of history and nostalgia.

"I know, and I understand how hard it is for you to admit that I'm right, too. Now, get your cute little ass inside that house, or I'm coming down to Florida. Tonight." Nelle talks a big game. She currently has a job being the boss babe she is at a mortgage firm, raking in the dough. With how hot the housing market is, she's raking in the cash. The peanut butter to my jelly. We each work differently yet hard at the same time. So, as much as she threatens to come down here, her job would never allow her to take any time off on a whim. The only chance I'll have my best friend here is if she takes a vacation, which she won't. Nelle is a workaholic through and through. Her number-one focus is work. The only person who can pull her away from it is me, and sadly, even me needing her in Florida right now would make her feel like she was being pulled in both directions. I'm not going to add that pressure to her plate. I'll suck it up somehow, even if I'm a needy friend and monopolize her time with phone calls or FaceTime calls.

"You're funny. We both know the mortgage firm would die if you upped and left on a whim." Nelle blows out a breath of air, like she's exasperated with her job when we all know the girl loves her work, her boss, and the company as a whole. "I'm okay now. Thank you for getting me through this. I'll call back if I can't make it into the actual house this time, okay?"

"Whatever you need, Tulsa, I'm here. We've got each other's backs. Forever," she replies as I stand up.

"Forever," I reply our motto. When she went through the hardest thing a woman ever should, it was me who held her hand the entire time, sleeping in her bed with her, wiping away the tears as her body rejected something she had no idea she'd truly want.

"Love you, Tulsa."

"I love you, too." I hit the end button and place my phone in my back pocket, feeling marginally better after the pep talk Nelle gave me. A smile crosses my face for the first time today, the dread that was sitting inside me slowly dissipates, and just as I'm turning around, ready to head inside, a voice comes from around the corner. A voice that I know like the back of my hand, making me second-guess every single thought I only just overcame.

"Tulsa Rose, what are you doing here?" I take a deep breath before turning toward Ledger Sinclair, completely unprepared to see him after all this time.

2

LEDGER

"She's back and about thirty minutes out from the house," Flay, the Williams' family attorney, told me when I answered the phone. No pleasantries were necessary, only the fact that I had to step off a job site, ask my employee to take over, then leave. I had to get home and let Tulsa in her own damn house. My roofing company hit the ground running the year after Montgomery passed away and Tulsa was at school. It got even bigger, needing more of my attention, when she told me how she really felt. There's not a day that goes by that I wish her brother were still alive. I'd gladly take his place if I could. Which is probably why I worked my ass off, trying to drown out all the memories, the mistakes I've made by sending her away even if it's what Montgomery wanted. Clearly, it was a fuckup considering it's taken her ten years to get her ass back to Orange Blossom.

The one thing you couldn't prepare yourself for happens before my eyes. Hearing what I heard made me want to turn around, travel back through the path from her place to mine, get in my truck, and drive like the flames of hell are on my ass. Tulsa Rose is just as pretty as she was the last time she was standing where she is now. The only difference is that the confidence she exudes now wasn't there last time.

"I'm pretty sure it's self-explanatory since this is my home, Ledger Sinclair." The full effect of her beauty shouldn't surprise me. It wasn't that long ago I was in the same town as her. Tulsa had no idea, and I'm not going to tell her. I take her in, my eyes drawn to her face at first, clear hazel eyes shooting daggers my way, soft kissable lips, a redness tinging her cheeks, whether that's from a happiness to see me or anger, I'm not sure. Her long soft brown hair flows down in soft wavy curls to her waist. She used to prefer to keep it in its natural form even when she was a teenager. I see not much has changed, including her preferred jean shorts, this pair is a dark wash, a light pink tank top, and her legs are bare besides the sandals on her feet.

"You haven't called this place home in a lot of years. You'll have to forgive me for not knowing I'd need to get off work to meet you here." Her back goes ramrod straight, hip cocked out. A light tap of her foot is the only hint of annoyance she gives away that I've hit a nerve.

"No one said you had to be here. I have a key of my own." I walk up the steps of the wraparound porch, making my way closer, watching as her eyes take me in. Probably because I'm filthy from the half day at work I was doing, tearing roofing materials off an old house. It makes for dirty work. The shirt I'm wearing is stained no matter how many times I've washed it. Same with my jeans, a few holes adding to the mix, and my boots are well worn.

"It won't work. I changed the locks last year." I don't tell her that the cleaning lady started poking around, and I caught her slipping something into her pocket. Confronting her wasn't going to do any good. So, I called Judd, the now Sheriff. He knew the deal with the Williams' house. By the time he walked inside, the woman was as white as a ghost. I didn't have her arrested. She emptied her pockets, left, and I called the cleaning service to cancel their service from then on out. I changed the locks, found a different service, and everything's been fine since then.

"Why would you do that?" I walk closer to her, hand sliding inside my pocket, digging out the key and ring.

"I wasn't sure when you'd be back. Figured I may as well, just in case." If Tulsa weren't projecting the *hands off* vibe, I'd be wrapping her in my arms and soaking in the girl who has become a woman. A lot of regrets are churning in my mind. My mother, damn her, she knew I'd feel them when Tulsa finally returned.

"I'll take those keys from you, then." She walks toward me, meeting me in the middle. There's a hesitance in us. I'm feeling like I'm walking on eggshells. I've kept to myself, going so far as to keeping my phone number away from her in order for her not to have to deal with me. After she called me, raging, crying, sobbing in the middle of the night, it pulled at my gut. It's why I was in my truck heading to Alabama, needing to see her, to know where her head was at and if she meant it. The smile plastered on her face told me she was healing, moving forward. Maybe I was the past holding her back. The change in phone number happened at the right time, cutting off all communication with her hurt, but it was better for her. It's not like she couldn't have called Flay to get my new number or look it up online. I like to call it the perfect storm. I was changing phone providers along with my number for my roofing company, Sinclair Roofing, when everything went down.

"How long are you staying?" I ask. Tulsa's palm is up. I make it a point to brush the tips of my fingers along her skin while dropping the keys into her upturned hand.

"Not that it's any business of yours, but I'm here to stay permanently. This is my home after all, and you're no longer my guardian." Her fingers tighten around the keys and keychain. I wonder if she sees what's attached to the key.

"Good. You were never meant to stay away for a decade, butterfly." I use the name she earned long ago, fluttering about every which way, unsure where she was going to land. It seems Tulsa Rose has finally found her wings.

"I can't do this right now. It was good to see you, but I've got things to do before next week. I'll see you around, Ledger." I've got no one to blame but myself for her aloofness. Even though giving up isn't an option, right now isn't the time to push. I can see this is going to take a toll on her. She's not been home in ten years. The place is still untouched, everything in its place like it was the last time she was here. If we had a better relationship, I'd walk inside with her, but since that's not the case, I'll take up residence out here. I already heard her tell someone she loves them on the phone. It caused an ache to settle in my chest, like one I haven't experienced, more so than the one time a year when it's the anniversary of Montgomery's death. A bottle of liquor stays in my hand the entire day while I sit in our old tree fort his father built for us when were kids and I've maintained throughout the years.

One thing is for certain about the Williams family—when they love you, it's deeply rooted. Like a tree that's been planted decades and decades ago, there's no uprooting it and letting go.

"I'll stay here all the same, unless you want me to start

unpacking your car for you?" I ask. If Tulsa could breathe fire like a dragon, she would be right about now. She looks like steam is about to blow out of her ears. "Or not." I throw my hands in the air while moving backwards until I'm leaning against the post, one ankle crossed over the other, my arms folded over my chest. Two can play this game. In most games, there's only one winner, but in ours, we'll both come out on top.

"I've been on my own enough that I can handle this without you hovering over me. Besides, if I need anything, I know who not to call, and that's you, Ledger." With that, she turns on her heel, hair whipping around as she sways her hips, doing nothing for another part of my body that's tightening—my damn cock.

"Not anymore, butterfly, not any-fucking-more," I tell to her retreating back, a promise I'm going to keep, and you can take that to the bank.

3

TULSA ROSE

You're doing it again, pushing him away like you did last time, and what did that do? Nothing. It did absolutely nothing even if I thought it was great idea at the time. *It just sucked that when you tried to make things right, he knocked down your attempt,* I think to myself. I open the screen door and slide the key inside the lock, all while the wooden screen door behind me is being held with my leg that's bent at the knee to keep it from slamming into my ankles. A trick I've used since I was a kid, hurrying inside to meet curfew or when you get home after a day at school and have to pee so bad, you're doing a dance. It's when the lock glides to the left, and the deadbolt slides away from the heavy wooden door that I see the glimmering lights flashing like a kaleidoscope. Looking down, I see the butterfly keychain Ledger handed me. Why would he give me something that's so memorable if he had no problem blocking me from his life? It still remains a mystery, and as much as I'd love to dissect everything that encompasses Ledger Sinclair, I do not have the time right now.

I am strong, I am brave, I am loved, and I can do this, I repeat the mantra in my head this time instead of out loud. My hand engulfs the doorknob, twisting it while using my other hand to push the door open, knowing the wood door swells if there was a heavy thunderstorm recently. Since this is Florida, the chances are high.

"Careful. The door is fixed," Ledger says as I almost go barreling through the doorway, ass over elbows.

"Now you tell me?" I look over my shoulder, taking another step inside, the screen door slamming behind me.

"You know now. That's good enough." A smooth-talking stranger is what Ledger has become, and damn if that's not a crying shame. I refocus on what's in front instead of what's behind me and take a deep breath of air. The scent of my childhood home triggers memories like they happened only yesterday. How I kissed my mom goodbye her last morning alive, how Daddy went to bed one night in his hunting cabin and never woke up, or how Montgomery kissed the top of my head and told me if I was leaving the house to send him a text, he was going out to meet with a friend, without me realizing it would be the last time I'd ever see them. It still smells like home, it still looks like home, it still feels like home, and I had no idea how much I missed it until now. I take a few more steps inside. Everything is the same, yet it has all changed. My feet take me to the living room, straight to the fireplace mantle where there are pictures of us throughout the years. The happy and loving family smiles back at me. For the first time in a long time, I know this is where I'm meant to be. It doesn't take me long to take a tour through the house, knowing I've got a lot of tedious tasks ahead of me. Montgomery took over our parents' room a year or so after Dad had passed, stripped it down to bare bones, replaced the flooring, remodeled the bathroom, and then made it his own. The few pieces of furniture we kept of our parents were moved to different areas of the house; everything else was donated. The kitchen still has the same charm from when it was built, Mom preserving it through the years we lived here, then it was Mont and myself doing the same. The only upgrades were the appliances. Still, I stood my ground, making sure he didn't go overboard on some kind of ridiculous space-like-looking gadget. I guess the plus side of leaving everything here and having Ledger and Mr. Flay take care of everything is that I've got a ready-made home. All I'll need to do is unpack my clothes, add to the frames on the mantle, then head into town to figure out food. The rest I can tackle in the next week or so before I start work. I'm walking up the stairs, hand trailing along the wood handrail. The light shining across the staircase makes it light and airy. The dark mahogany floors, the trim, the doors are all in the same stain. This house is what made me want to become the interior designer I am today, working with others to showcase a house in its prime, bringing it back to life for generations to come and enjoy it. I bypass the second-floor bathroom, my bedroom, and what is now the guest bedroom, and move to Montgomery's room. After he passed away, for a week straight this is where you could find me. I didn't talk unless it was to Ledger. I didn't eat unless he made me, which was often, and even then, there wasn't an appetite to be had. I'd grab the blanket from the foot of the bed, wrap it tightly around my body and head, like we used to do after the world seemed to be so heavy with grief, when Mont was the one who held what was left of our family together. The tears cascade down my cheeks uncontrollably as I open his door, walk inside, and collapse onto his bed once again. The blanket is up and over my body, head beneath it as well as I let the tears take over. I'm allowing myself this one last time to grieve through the process of being home, then I'm going to get up, clean myself up, and get things squared away. Right now, this is what I need more than ever, a cathartic cleansing. As my therapist says, it's okay to be sad, mad, or any other emotion as long as you don't unpack those feelings and live there. I close my eyes, not worrying about the man I left downstairs, the one who still has me in a state of riotous emotions: want, need, desire, love, it's all there. When I lost my virginity with a boy my second year of college, no longer sharing a dorm with three other girls, that is, it was to a vision of Ledger, his heat and body surrounding me. And the boy was nothing to write home about. God, it was horrible. Thankfully, after telling my best friend what happened, Nelle marched us right to a store and helped me pick out a toy. Let's just say I was opened to a whole new world— different shapes, sizes, colors, some that vibrate, suction to the shower wall, and then there's my choice favorite, bright pink in color, the two rabbit ears thrumming my clit as the dildo moves counter-clockwise or clockwise as you reach your orgasm. It was ten times better than the one college boy experience I had. He only wanted a piece of my body to throw me away the next day. Been there, done that, saw it many times over during my college life. How I made it a full year without calling Mr. Flay and begging to find me off campus housing, I have no idea.

My eyes flutter closed. The drive from Alabama to Orange Blossom, Florida took a toll on my body, as well as the emotions, and I slowly drift to sleep, feeling a contentment I haven't felt in too many years to count. Nelle was right after all—coming home is exactly what I needed. If only I can convince her to move here, too.

4

LEDGER

Tulsa never came back out, not in the twenty minutes I waited while going through emails on my phone, responding to the text messages that have piled up. The calls are the one thing I won't be returning. Getting wrangled into an hour-long conversation with a potential client or my secretary asking questions non-stop is not what I need right now. I almost assumed she'd come flying out the door. I should have known better; the girl has more grit than anyone I know. I've seen that for myself on the two days a month I would allow myself to travel to Alabama, showing me that she was thriving, exactly what Montgomery wanted even if I had to be the bad guy. It was hard as hell watching her live a life without me. Seeing her tip her head up toward the sun, closing her eyes, and smiling, it about gutted me. The same thing Tulsa did when she would step outside on the back deck before going in the pool.

"Fuck it." I've waited long enough. If she's in that house alone, falling apart, she's going to do it on me, even if I'm the

reason she's breaking down. I fling open the screen door.
Since she left the front door wide open, it's enough of an
invite to come inside. My eyes were watching the long-
haired beauty the entire time, noticing that she went up the
stairs. That's the way I head. I don't notice anything different
in the house. No upgrades were necessary, and she would
have had my head if I'd changed one single fucking thing
without okaying it in the process. The only things I've done
have been maintenance—a leaky faucet, the pool pump
that's in desperate need to be replaced but I've been Band-
Aiding back together for the time being, and replacing the
wood steps on the side of the house. This year, I was going to
talk to Flay about painting the outside. A few spots are being
beaten to death by the hot Florida sun. Since Tulsa is home
now, it'll move up on the maintenance schedule.

I stop at the door to her bedroom. It's closed, but she
could still be in there. I don't bother knocking. Tulsa Rose's
room is the exact same way she's had it since she and Mrs.
Williams decorated it before she passed away. The walls are
still a dusty rose. The metal headboard with white bedding,
an addition she's made through the years, and light wood
dresser and nightstand complete the bulk of the furniture. I
step inside. Not seeing her anywhere in the room, I back out
of it and close the door behind me. The guest room she'd
never be in; there's no reason. I bypass the bathroom and hit
pay dirt. Mont's bedroom door is flung open.

"Son of a bitch," I murmur quietly when I see the form of
a body beneath Mont's favorite blanket. I swear to Christ if
she's reverting to when Montgomery passed away, I'm going
to take my hand to her ass. Fuck, that has me thinking about
other things, things I damn well shouldn't be thinking, not at
a time like this. Light on my feet, which is damn near impos-

sible in steel-toed boots, I edge closer to the bed. I move my hand toward the mattress, grateful I had enough time to hurry home, wash up a little bit before making the trek by foot from my property to hers.

"Butterfly, it's time to come out of your cocoon." I carefully lift the blanket, holding my breath, preparing for the worst, hoping for the best. I slowly remove the blanket from the top until her face is showing, eyes squeezed shut, lashes fluttering along her cheeks. The streaks of mascara down her face tell me all I need to know. Tulsa Rose came in here, let her emotions take over, and fell asleep. A piece of me is tempted to move the blanket further down her body, slide beside her, and help her settle into a more peaceful sleep. The other part of me knows if she were to wake up with me beside her, I'd be in a world of fucking hurt. It seems we've both made some mistakes in our past, and even though her words ripped my world apart, she still needs me, even if she can't admit it to herself. "Sleep, butterfly," I tell her softly as my lips graze her forehead, leaving the blanket off her face unlike how she had it. I've got no idea how she was able to sleep like that. I'd suffocate without some kind of moving air. Montgomery and she would do this when their world was shaking, sadly too fucking much for either of them, but especially for Tulsa Rose. I take one last look over my shoulder on my way out the door, my hand going to my pocket, digging out my phone to shoot a text to my crew and secretary that I'd be off for the remainder of the day, a rarity since I only ever took a few days off once a month, though I still made myself available should something materialize. That's not going to happen today. As soon as I'm out of hearing distance, I take the steps just as fast as I did when my goal was to find Tulsa all the while texting who I need to before I throw my phone down on the table by the front door then head out front. We all live far enough off the beaten path that locking your car doors is unheard of, let alone your house. I'll have to make sure Tulsa does at least lock the doors in the house. The windows are a lost cause. Spring in Florida is either hot or cold, never in the middle like it has been this year, with warm days and cooler nights.

I'm at Tulsa's car in a few short minutes, opening up the back hatch of her SUV. Another thing that's pissed me off, she hasn't touched much of her trust fund. Since she worked her ass off in high school academically to pay for her tuition, all she had to use from what the Williams left her was room and board, working part-time for extras in the way of food when money was set aside for anything else. Damn stubborn Williams pride running through her blood. Hell, she didn't even touch her money to buy the new SUV I'm currently opening. One that Montgomery would wholeheartedly approve of, a Chevy Tahoe, black on black interior and exterior. I chuckle when I see the amount of shit she's got packed inside the back, boxes stacked one on top of the other. Both the second and third row seats are down, and every square inch is filled.

"Some things never change." Tulsa has everything labeled—clothes, books, toiletries. Nice and organized. Considering the weight of the first box, I'm going to get a different type of workout today besides climbing up and down ladders to work on a roof or the gym I have at my house. I go back and forth, bringing one box in after the other, propping the screen door open while doing so until all of them are in the house. Tulsa can always unpack them from here in the living room and carry what she needs up the stairs. She won't ask for any help from me, preferring to do it all on her own.

Once the last box is off-loaded, I see her keys are on the counter. It doesn't take me long to open the junk drawer and grab the notepad inside along with a pen. This way, when or if she wakes up, she will notice the boxes are in the house. Her vehicle, and the house will be locked up. I may have given her a new set of house keys, but I still have the other set.

Butterfly,

I hope you slept well. Don't carry the boxes up the stairs. I'll help you once I'm back from town with groceries.

Ledger

I WALK out the door and turn around to lock it, knowing there's a woman inside who's still grieving the loss of her family and needing her to be safe.

5

TULSA ROSE

I wake up and swear the smell of Ledger is lingering in my brother's room, but that can't be. Ledger wouldn't willingly come inside, not when I pushed him away for the second time in only the handful of times we've spoken since that fateful day. Okay, fine. We've yet to talk since I was a complete and total bitch to him. Who wishes someone else would take the place of their dead brother? That's so wrong. And while I apologized in a two-page letter that was returned to me unopened, it was me who broke the line of communication in the first place. That still doesn't explain why I'm smelling the cologne that embodies Ledger Sinclair. I blink away the sleep and roll over onto my back, which is another thing. Usually when I wake up beneath the blanket fort I make for myself, my whole body is covered up. That wasn't the case and is probably why I'm waking up when I feel like I could have slept at least another hour.

My body protests the thought of getting up, so I take the time to stretch, arms going over my head, neck moving from side to side, my legs straightening, toes pointing, eyes closing, feeling that dizzying effect you get when you've held a pose too long, before I finally decide to get out of my brother's bed. The scent of him has long since passed; it's the feeling of comfort, of knowing that when I was having a rough day on the anniversary of one of our parents' deaths, a boy breaking my heart, or school was kicking my ass in the math department, Mont would make it better. We'd hide away. I'd cry on his shoulder, and he'd make the pain go away, even if it was only for a moment.

"Time to get your lazy ass out of bed. You've got a truck to unpack, groceries to buy, and things to figure out, Tulsa Rose," I tell the empty room before I flip to my side and move off the bed, taking the blanket with me. It might have been Montgomery's favorite blanket, but it's also mine, and there's no way I'm going to stay in our family home without it in my room. I bundle the blanket up in a ball, smooth the comforter out, and walk toward the bedroom that's always been mine. Mont offered me the master bedroom once everything settled down a couple of years after Dad had passed away. I didn't want to leave my bedroom; it was perfect for me. Still is. The window seat Dad built with the bookshelves on either side is utter perfection to look out on a pretty day or starry night, and honestly, I'm not sure I'd ever move into the master bedroom anyways. Call it a superstition, but the last three people who lived in that room are no longer here.

I close the door on my way out and head to my bedroom, open the door, and leave it that way, throwing the blanket on the bed on my way to do the same to the windows. I probably should open the house and let it air out while I'm unpacking my truck. Then, by the time I head into town to grab some groceries, the house will have fresh spring air flowing through it instead of the smell of a house that's been closed up for too long.

Once that's done, I move to the bathroom I'll be using, open the window there, too, then turn on the water in the bathtub, something I really should have done before taking a nap. I'm sure the cleaning company uses the water, probably not as much as I will, a hot bath in the oversized tub, and when you're on well water, this is a necessity to run, especially since that's what I'll be using as soon as things are settled. I look at the clock. I slept less than an hour. Damn, I really wish my body had allowed me to sleep a smidge longer.

As I make my way down the stairs, I notice the front door is closed and locked, a sign of Ledger's handy work for sure because never in my life has my front door been locked when I've lived here. Shut, yes. The Florida heat and humidity are real, hot as hell nine or ten months out of the year. The seasons go from hot to hotter, to hotter than Satan's butthole to cool with a freeze here or there in between, and then were back to hot. My feet hit the last step before I'm off the stairs, shock hitting my body like a cold-water plunge when I see the boxes set up nice and neat.

"Jesus, I do not deserve this. I'm an asshole. Every freaking interaction I have with Ledger, I become a bigger bitch." I walk toward the boxes, my hand sliding along the top of them, then head to the kitchen, where I see my car keys are sitting right next to the key and keychain he gave me. The note beneath it is from Ledger. I run my fingers through my hair while reading it, heart squeezing in my chest, and still, I don't have his number to call or text him to say thank you. I guess that means he's coming back. The only thing I can do now is sit and wait. Well, there is running water in the bathtub that could go to good use. With that thought in mind, I quickly scan the boxes, find the one I need, and rip the top open to grab the body wash, hair clip, and razor. I close it back up to dig through the next box, finding a comfortable lounge set Nelle bought me as my coming home gift. The color compliments my skin tone with its light pink hue, and it's got bell-style sleeves and flares in the softest fabric one could ever feel against your body. God, I miss her already, and it's barely been eight hours. I head back upstairs, leaving the boxes where they are. My phone is in my room, after tossing it on the bed along with Mont's blanket. I could call or text Nelle, tell her what I'm feeling and what Ledger did, but I'm not ready to open that can of worms yet. I'll do that tomorrow when I don't run the risk of him walking back into my house and catching me on the phone talking about him. No thanks.

"God, I've missed this bathtub." Talking out loud is my jam. Others have a different vice, like going out and drinking, a shoe or clothes weakness, spending in some sort of capacity. Mine is talking to no one in particular except to myself. That and spending as much time outside as possible. I slip out of my clothes, drop them in a pile on the floor, kick them off to the side with my foot, grab my claw clip to bunch my long hair on top of my head, plug the tub since the water has run clear, pour a healthy capful of the all-natural body wash, another favor from Nelle and our time together, and then I slide into the hot water, allowing the warmth to wash all of my worries away.

6

LEDGER

"**Y**ou look like you're stocking up for the first time ever, Ledger," Mrs. Marble states as I'm loading up the last of the groceries I picked up at the local store. At first, I was only going to get a few things to last her through the day and tomorrow, then thought better of it. There's no food at all at Tulsa's house. Not even a seasoning was left behind. She wasn't going to be home, and instead of letting it go to waste, I had the cleaning service box it all up to donate everything to the local food pantry that wasn't expired.

"Tulsa's home. I figure she needs some food for a bit," I tell her, grabbing the last few bags.

"Honey, that's enough to last her a few weeks, let alone days. You're a good man, Ledger Sinclair." She pats my arm. I look at the back of my truck—paper towels, toilet paper, coffee, creamer, breakfast items, stuff to make sandwiches, because as far back as I can remember, Tulsa has always loved a good turkey and provolone sandwich with chips inside it, pickles stacked high in between. And then there are a few things she can make for dinner—fried chicken, mashed potatoes, the fixings for salads.

"Thank you, Mrs. Marble. I suppose you're going to call my momma and let her know Tulsa is back in town and you just so happened to see me at the grocery store?" She's one of the town busybodies, older in age, a widow herself. You've got to love small town living—everyone knows you, and there's no going somewhere without bumping into someone.

"You'd be right about that. I'll also be telling her how well raised you are." It's then I notice she's pushing her own cart full of groceries. With my truck loaded with everything for Tulsa, I close the door and walk her toward her car.

"That's a good thing, I suppose. Let me help you load your groceries." It won't take more than a few minutes, and I know she struggles with lifting the gallons of water she buys especially for her inside cat.

"You're a dear. Now tell me, are you going to let Tulsa leave Orange Blossom again?" She holds on to my bicep as we walk the few cars down from mine until we arrive at hers.

"Noticed that, did you?" We stop in the middle of the path, me looking down at her as a sly smile alights her face.

"I see everything. You're not answering my question, young man." She opens the trunk to her car. I evade the subject for as long as I can until I've packed the few bags and jugs of water in her trunk, closing it when I'm done. Mrs. Marble is still standing there, keys in her hand, waiting for my response.

"Nope, I'm not letting her go. Montgomery might be rolling over in his grave or cussing me up a storm. I sent her off for her own good. She needed to get out of this town. Everyone would have only questioned her to death, driving her crazy. Mom may not have agreed with sticking to Mont's last will and testament, but I had to do it. Not just for Tulsa but for myself, too," I admit. Shit, the feelings I was having for her were not something I'd allow myself to navigate. The temptation, though, it had me worried about myself, and no way was I fucking around with her while she was not only underage, but she was also grieving. I'm an asshole, but not that much of one.

"Like I said, you're a good man, Ledger. Thank you for loading my groceries. Go get to your girl. Something tells me she'll need a meal here before too long." I dip my head, kiss her cheek, and squeeze her hand.

"Thank you, Mrs. Marble. I'll see you around." I leave her to get settled in the car. She's right. Tulsa is probably starving, if she's awake. Both she and her brother could sleep well into the day, not waking up until noon if they could get away with it. Tulsa was always the napper, though, on the lounge outside by the pool, in her window seat in her room after reading a magazine on some kind of home design, or in the living room on the couch while watching television.

I'm in my truck, seatbelt buckled and turning over the engine when my cell phone starts ringing. I look at the dash. It's Ella, my secretary. I hit the end button on my steering wheel. She's going to learn when I say I'm unavailable for the remainder of the day, that's exactly what I mean. Damn, we've had this conversation a few times now. On the trips to Alabama, she'd call me over something mundane that my foreman could have answered, and now who the fuck knows what she wants. I tune it out, all of it, and turn the radio on, getting lost in the music as I make the trek back to Tulsa's. A fifteen-minute ride along the near empty highway doesn't take a lot of time. I will say as I pull onto the road that leads to my house and Tulsa's, I kind of expected a phone call from my mother. Not receiving one has my hackles raised. You never know when a mother hen comes out to shake her tail feathers. My mom lives closer to town. I bought my house in my early twenties when it came up for sale before shit went sideways and I lost my best friend. Mom oftentimes questioned what I was doing after that happened but never gave unsolicited advice, only asked if I was sure that was what I should be doing. I drive past my long driveway, head to the Williams, and turn in. After a few winding curves, trees overhanging the dirt driveway, I'm parking beside her Tahoe. At least she didn't get up and leave the house; that's a plus in my book. I put my Ford F-250 diesel in park; I need it to pull the trailers when I'm on a jobsite. I don't bother to bring my phone, keys in one hand to unlock the front door to the house and opening the back door of my truck to grab as many bags of groceries I can to take care of it in one trip. I can come back and grab the nonperishable stuff later. My main focus is on getting inside and checking on Tulsa. A few moments of intense juggling of opening the screen door, sliding the key into the deadbolt, pushing the bags in before my body so they don't get stuck between the two doors, and I'm inside. The heel of my foot closes it. Only the quiet greets me, so I move toward the kitchen to put the bags of food on the counter, sorting through what goes in the fridge. Tulsa will no doubt sort through it and organize it the way she wants. The girl and her organization skills is one that still boggles my brain.

I'm making my way out of the kitchen, taking the steps, ready to check on her, even if I know she's more than likely still fast asleep in Montgomery's bed. I should have realized the lighting is different, that there's a breeze floating down the stairs. When I hit the landing and come upon the bathroom, the door more than ajar, the scent of spun sugar makes me stop and look inside.

"Butterfly." Her head is tipped back, eyes closed, hair piled up on top. The slope of her neck is arched, one long leg is on the ledge, water dripping down, and when she lets out a low moan from the back of her throat, I know exactly what her hands are doing beneath the water.

7

TULSA ROSE

"Ledger." His name that has always left my lips when I'm making myself come slides along my skin like a whisper. The bathroom softly echoes my moan. I swear there's a hint of his cologne permeating the air again, and with my eyes closed, imagining that it's Ledger's long thick fingers sliding along the lips of my pussy seems very real. I push one finger inside, the walls of my center clamping down like a vise around the digit. In my not so real reality, he's sitting in front of me, his legs spreading me open, his fingers inside, two of them, generous in the way he hits that area in an upturned way, hitting my G-spot when in fact the only time that has ever happened is when I'm using my toy. I slide another finger inside, head tipping back, breasts moving out of the water, the cooler air making my nipples pebble harder than they were beneath the surface.

"Butterfly." I could have sworn I heard it earlier, thinking it was all in my head. This time, I know I heard it. My thumb slides along my clit as I hear the footsteps getting closer, the thud of heavy boots walking along the hardwood floors. My eyes fly open, not for a second thinking that Ledger would actually come into the bathroom. My fingers stop what they're doing, unsure on how to navigate this moment. "Don't stop on my account." There, in the flesh, unlike my imagination, Ledger is standing over me, in the same clothes he was wearing earlier—well-worn, perfectly molded to his tall muscular build. I watch as the toe of his boot grabs the small wooden stool, moving it without taking his eyes off me. Eyes that are currently sweeping along the whole of my body, from my eyes that I'm sure are blazing with desire, lingering on my chest, to my legs, to the knee up against the side of the tub, the other splayed open and on the edge of the porcelain beneath my body. The heat in his gaze is full of lust and adoration. We're both feeling the same thing even if he does hate me because of a ton of unresolved issues. Talk about a lot of baggage. The clenching of his jaw tells me he wants to watch me as I come with him as he's sitting beside me on the outside of the tub.

"Ledger?" I pose a question, knowing this probably isn't one of the brightest ideas we've ever had. His big body dwarfs the stool beneath him. One hand dips beneath the water, gathering the bubbles, to slide along my inner thigh. My flesh lights on fire beneath the tips of his fingers.

"Keep going, Tulsa Rose, let me watch you fuck yourself." His voice leaves no room to argue, deep, dark, and demanding. It's kind of hard not to do what he says, even if my mind is telling me this isn't a great idea. Tell that to my traitorous body that takes the opportunity to arch further into the ministrations of my own hand, thumb moving in slow smooth circles, breast in full view of Ledger's sight now that my breathing is becoming more erratic. My eyes stay on his as I tunnel my fingers in and out of my slick depths, the water rippling with every movement.

"Ledger, I'm so close." Unable to keep my eyes on his, I tip my head back, feeling the pressure of his hands, the indents from the tips of his fingers, and if I'm lucky, I'll be wearing the bruises from Ledger as he holds himself back.

"The next time you come, Tulsa Rose, it'll be with my fingers, my head buried between your soft-as-hell thighs, and when we get to the point where we once were, it'll be my cock." That's all it takes. His words, my fingers, the sensation of his hands on my body, and I'm tipping over the edge.

"Oh God, Ledger," I moan, wishing it were him doing all the work. Just once when I get off, I'd like it to be the real deal. Not a silicone toy, not a man who took his place for all of two minutes as I was trying to keep him out of my mind, body, and soul. It seems that's impossible, though, because Ledger Sinclair is permanently ingrained in every part of me.

"Fuck, that was pretty. I'm leaving before I take something you're not ready for yet. Come downstairs when you're done with your bath," Ledger states. My eyes open, and I watch as he stands up, the bulge in his jeans showing me how big he truly is after only feeling him pressed against me a handful of times. It causes my center to spasm again, protesting at the fact that I'm pulling my fingers away from myself. Greedy is the one word I'd describe what I'm feeling right about now.

"Okay." I'm breathless, chest still heaving, trying to get my breathing under control. Ledger stands there still watching me, seeing what I'll do next, I'm sure. I surprise myself as I slide my leg back inside the tub, plant my feet in the tub beneath me, and use my hands on the ledge to lift myself up. The water has long since cooled off. The breeze from the open window raises goose bumps along my feverish skin.

"Christ, butterfly, you're not playing fair. I'll see you downstairs." He licks his lips, top and bottom, in a way that you only see in a movie, long and slow, dragging the process out. It makes you want to taste and feel them against yours. I stay planted where I am. It'd be so easy to step out of the tub and run into his arms. Sadly, Ledger is right. There are so many things we need to talk about. An apology he more than deserves from me, and answers to the pile of questions I have. He walks out the door. I shuffle my feet until I can push the stopper that's holding the water out of its plug, allowing the water to drain. The bubbles from the makeshift bubble bath slide off my skin. I reach for the towel on the vanity and catch sight of my body in the mirror. I'm flushed, cheeks rosy, chest much the same. I know I need to get my butt dried off, clothed, and down the stairs, but damn if I'm not nervous. So many variables are running through my mind that I have half a mind to stay sequestered upstairs, hiding out like a teenage girl throwing a temper tantrum after being late from curfew. That's not what I'm going to do, though. Instead, I dry my body off and go through the rest of the motions, cleaning up after myself, semi-prolonging the process until I can't anymore. It's time to put one foot in front of the other and figure out what the hell is going on between Ledger and me.

8

LEDGER

My cock is going to have a permanent zipper imprint after witnessing the hottest fucking thing of my life. I've got zero regrets walking in on her and watching as she got herself off, especially because it was with the thought of me before I even made my presence known. The only thing I'm currently upset with is the fact I didn't catch Tulsa taking care of herself on her bed. I've got some fantasies a man should never have had when she was seventeen years old and I was twenty-seven. It's a damn good thing I never acted on them because one thing's for sure: if Montgomery had found out while he was still alive, I'd be the one dead instead of him. I walk out the house, grab the paper products out of my truck, and check my phone to make sure nothing pressing needs my attention. Ella called and texted again, about some issue on a purchase order. I leave it where it is. That shit can wait, and there are other people at the office who can work on it. When I first started my roofing company, the yard and small trailer office were at the back of my property. That shit quickly changed when workers were coming and going too damn much, tearing up my yard to get to the back of the property. A man needs some damn peace and quiet away from work. The next year, I secured an office space with a bigger yard, where I am able to keep more materials on-hand. Having that shit away from my house gave me exactly what I needed.

"Hey, you really went all out," Tulsa greets me as I struggle to open the screen door. Damn nuisance of a door. She holds the door open for me, my body sliding against hers as I pass. Our breaths hitch. Yep, my cock is never going to recover from today.

"Figured you'd be too tired to go into town, deal with all the questions after driving seven hours," I tell her. It's the truth. Once the town gets wind that Tulsa Rose is back, she's going to be bombarded with hugs, questions, and a meal train of sorts all over again. This way, she can ease herself into it at her own pace.

"I don't deserve this." Her eyes lower, lashes fanning her cheeks, shoulders slumping.

"Hey, none of that. Give me your eyes, butterfly," I tell her. Since my hands are full, the door is still propped open with her hand, I wait to continue until she's opened her eyes and lifted her head so she can look at me while I'm talking to her. "We'll get through this. Right now, we're going to go to the kitchen, put the rest of the groceries away, eat the fried chicken, mashed potatoes, and salad I picked up, see what's on television, then go from there, alright?"

"That will work. I'm going to repay you, and I already know you won't take my money, so I'll have to figure some-thing out. Need help?" she asks.

"Nope. You can start on organizing the food. Basically

threw it all in the fridge when I came back. My priority was checking on you. I wasn't too thrilled with the déjà vu scene when I saw you in Mont's bed, butterfly." We make our way into the kitchen. She's trailing behind me. Shit, my chest tightens at seeing the way she was tucked beneath the big brown blanket.

"Nope, not reverting to those days. It was more of a purge than anything. Coming back home was a lot to take in, memories hitting me all at once, realizing how much I missed my home and the town. I hope you realize I'm here to stay." I plop the paper products on the counter, hip leaning on it as I watch Tulsa move throughout the kitchen, opening the bags, watching as she takes out her number-one vice in the food department: pickles. The girl has always had a love for them—spicy, dill, sweet, loaded with garlic, it doesn't matter. I know she prefers her favorite pickles from a local farmer, and if I had time, I would have swung by their stand to pick them up. Of course then I'd be questioned to death, they'd know Tulsa was back in town, and her phone would start ringing off the hook.

"You remembered?" Four jars are wrapped in her arm as she carries them to the fridge.

"How could I not? It wasn't me who gave you that awful nickname." I'm referring to Montgomery's name he gave her before I knew both of them. I was a transplant in middle school, Mom being a widow at a young age, my father gone too early because of a war.

"Ugh, don't even say it. I may love pickles, which came in handy during my college days—talk about instant rehydration—but Pickle Girl is not the name anyone wants to be called behind closed doors or in public." She opens the refrigerator door, grimacing at the disarray I left it in.

"I imagine you wouldn't. Sorry, my mind wasn't on the fridge." I shrug my shoulders then move in behind her to start taking the rest of the groceries out of the bags. The essentials were all that mattered, along with the beer.

"I'd have redone it anyway." She puts things where she wants it, and I hand her the rest of the shit that needs to be put away. She hands me a bottle of beer, then another. It seems Tulsa will be joining me in having a drink.

"I know, that's why I didn't bother. You ready to eat?" I open the beers and place hers on the counter.

"Food, or I'm going to be drunk after two beers. I really don't have time to nurse a hangover. I've got less than a week before I start my job. Tomorrow, I'm working around the house. If there's anything you noticed that needs to be taken care of that you haven't already, that'd be awesome. It's time I've boxed some things up, donate and whatnot." I grab the plates from the cabinet as she pulls the food out of the fridge; she's still fiddling with the organization. I didn't buy too much of food for the pantry, so she'll eventually have to focus on it, but for now, I open up the package of fried chicken, the mashed potatoes, then start working on plating our food.

"Not a bad idea. The only thing on the plans this year was painting the outside of the house and figuring out the pool situation," I tell her.

"What's wrong with the pool?"

"The pool pump needs to be replaced. It's been a chlorine pool for a while; it'd be cheaper on chemicals and easier to maintain if you transition to a salt pool. The sun just eats at the chlorine and tablets. I didn't want to do that big of a task until Flay talked to you, but since you're home, we can get the ball rolling with whatever you decide." She closes the fridge door and moves close. I pull her in front of me while I finish up our plates. My arms are around her body, both of us pressed together, and while we need to talk, I'd rather it didn't happen tonight. She has enough on her plate.

"That makes sense. I'd rather go with salt if it's going to be cheaper in the long run, plus you won't smell like chlorine when you get out. If you let me know the company names, I'll start getting quotes." She moves, her ass jutting against my cock. Damn thing has yet to go down since I've returned from the grocery store, a constant state of hardness with Tulsa Rose around.

"Butterfly, why would you pay a company when I'm the one who was going to install it in the first place?" She looks over her shoulder.

"I'd still pay you." I arch an eyebrow at her. Like fucking hell she will. "Yeah, yeah, whatever. One of these days."

"You want to pay me back, you can do it in a bikini while I'm working." I wink at her and watch her flush. I remember all too well the year she turned seventeen, how she'd make an excuse to walk by me in that red bikini of hers.

"Should I wear high heels while carrying a tray of sweet tea, too?" That smile of hers lights up her face.

"Fuck the heels, and I'd rather drink beer." I back away to grab the plates, moving away before I say fuck it, abandon the food, and have a different kind of meal than what we're about to eat.

"Good to know. I'm suddenly famished," she changes the subject. I drop it, a smirk on my face knowing that I'm getting to her. The feeling is entirely mutual.

9

TULSA ROSE

"Nelle, you won't believe what happened last night. I swear I'm getting whiplash," I tell her the next day while sitting on the floor in Montgomery's room, going through his clothes. A donate pile, a trash pile, and a keep pile all sit surround me. Sadly, or not so sadly, the donate pile is mammoth. The few pieces of clothing I'm keeping are a college crewneck sweatshirt and a few tee shirts he kept from his high school days. The rest, someone else could use, and honestly, I really thought this would be a lot harder than it is.

"Well, what are you waiting for? Tell me everything." She's sitting at her desk, tapping away at the keyboard, while I'm sorting through the rest of Mont's closet. On to shoes now, which will all be donated, minus his gym shoes. No one should ever be forced to go near them, me included.

"Ledger made his presence known. It was like the past was washed away. I mean, he's always been this dominant alpha type of male, but yesterday, he was like a completely different person. I fell asleep after making my rounds through the house. He left, and when I woke up, my boxes were unloaded," I tell her.

"Please tell me you're getting to the good part because right now, this a snooze fest." She pretends to yawn. I roll my eyes at her. My best friend is a drama queen.

"If you'd quit interrupting, I'd have told you already, but no," I hold up a rogue tee I found at the bottom of Mont's closet. "That's weird. This isn't Mont's; it's Ledgers, one I stole from him and kept in my bedroom. I wonder how it got in Montgomery's room, on the closet floor, buried in the back no less." Ledger had left one of his shirts here, giving me ample opportunity to pinch it, which I did, only wearing it to bed when Mont wasn't around. I got to wear it a handful of times before it disappeared. It broke my heart thinking I'd misplaced it. I set it aside. I'll be going back to my thoughts on how it ended up here later. "Anyways, I'm in the bathtub taking myself to pound town when he walks in, literally." Nelle moves her eyes away from the computer screen.

"No way. Please tell me he joined in on the fun."

"Kind of. He more or less watched, but man, oh man. I'm not sure I've ever come that hard before," I admit.

"Well, to be fair, your few experiences have sucked, and you rely heavily on your toy." Nelle has no room to talk. She's as selective as I am when it comes to who we share ourselves with.

"True, true. Anyways, we've yet to talk. We ate dinner together last night, then he left once it started getting dark out." I don't mention that falling asleep last night took hours. Concealer was my best friend this morning to hide the dark circles. The lack of rest could be from the nap I took or being back home, hearing the different noises or lack of noises out here compared to the apartment Nelle and I shared. Instead of tossing and turning, I emptied the boxes. Clothes and makeup were my priorities. I still need to figure out where I want to put everything else, as well as changing up the style now that this is my own home.

"Wow, a kiss good night at least?"

"Does it count if it's a brush against your forehead?" I respond, biting my lower lip. The answer doesn't even need to be spoken.

"Yeah, you know it doesn't. No wonder you're confused. I think you might have to confront this head-on." Nelle saying that only solidifies the answer to my question.

"No kidding. Everything going good for you?" I've dominated the conversation with my woe is me enough the past two days. Whereas my life has been inundated with one tragedy after the next, Nelle has both her parents, who were there for her as well as I was when her body rejected the pregnancy she wasn't sure she wanted. In the end, it broke a piece of her. Nelle had been there for me since Ledger dropped me off at our dorm room, so it was time for me to do the same. We rallied, leaned on one another, and slowly, she was able to smile again without feeling guilty.

"Ugh, don't get me started. Work is work, which is fine, but the chick who was going to move in and take your room backed out, literally, right before you called me." Shit, now I really feel bad. I know the apartment is expensive, even if I did leave her with a few months' rent to cushion the blow.

"Okay, don't hate me, but please tell me why you can't move here when you work remotely the majority of the time. I have two bedrooms here that are not doing anything except sitting empty." I've tried my hardest to convince her to move to Florida with me. She made up one excuse after excuse—work, the lease at the apartment, which I would have helped pay in order for her to leave with me. I mean, her parents are in Alabama, and if mine were still alive, I probably wouldn't move permanently either, but this way, she has a place for the time being until she knows what she wants to do.

"I know. I've been thinking on that, too. I'm going to see how the next month goes, talk to my parents, and make sure work is able to set up a secure line for me to do loan approvals in a different state. It's been less than twenty-four hours, and I'm being a clingy best friend." She scrunches up her face like it's a bad thing.

"Um, hello! The feeling is entirely mutual. Speaking from one clingy best to the other, am I not the one in this duo who is practically begging on my knees? There's a pool here, no kids, a few acres, which by the way, I'm going to do something I haven't done since I was a kid. And I could really use your help even if you don't get your hands dirty." There haven't been flowers in the yard since Mom passed away. I want to plant wildflowers, maybe a small vegetable garden. Of course, that's going to require some heavy lifting, building raised beds, along with some fencing because squirrels, rabbits, and deer would have no problem eating your crop as a snack.

"Are you trying to convince me to move or convince me to stay in Alabama?" Nelle jokes.

"You can stand there and look pretty. I'm about to have weekends free, and after Ledger works on the pool, and I get the outside of the house painted, I'm going to be pretty bored. So, why not start a garden of sorts?" I shrug my shoulders. Apartment living was nice at the time, but I couldn't imagine myself living in a city without a big yard to occupy my time.

"That's a great idea, since you left me with the tomatoes,

cucumbers, and bell peppers on the patio. I can't be held responsible for keeping them alive. You know what? Maybe moving is a bad idea. You have giant life-sucking mosquitos. Eww!"

"Okay, drama queen, the offer stands. I'm going to let you go to work and keep working out how things will go with Ledger. Call me later," I tell her.

"I will. Love you, and keep my posted. You sure you're okay?" This almost seems too easy for me, which makes me realize I either need to make an appointment with my therapist via Zoom, or I'm finally allowing myself to heal.

"I'm positive. You do the same. Love you, bestie!" I look around the floor, at the bags upon bags I need to lug downstairs.

"Love you." We each hang up, and I continue on my task, going through the rest of his bedroom, scrunching my nose at the box of expired condoms, wondering if I should ask Ledger to finish this task, except I'm no quitter, so I'll carry on, doing what I should have done years ago instead of being a coward and staying away.

10

LEDGER

"Yeah, I got the texts, the emails, and the damn phone calls. What was so important you deemed it necessary to put a 9-1-1 with it?" I walk into the office the next morning talking to Ella, my secretary, about the ridiculousness she's been starting. After I left Tulsa's and got home, I took care of a few things around the house before I grabbed a shower, where I jacked my cock to the memory of watching her fingering her pussy. Her tits were unbound, floating above the water, cherry-red nipples begging for my mouth, eyes falling closed then fluttering open when I spoke. Fuck, it was a beautiful sight to see. It took me no time at all to spray my cum on the shower floor, which did absolutely nothing to deflate my cock.

"You never go silent. We have orders to go over, appointments to get scheduled for estimates, and you ducked out of all of it yesterday." I take a sip of my coffee, annoyed after spending a great day with Tulsa going well into the evening. The only issue was saying goodbye to her, seeing the hurt in her eyes when I didn't give her what she wanted. The only reason I didn't get a taste of her lips is because when I start, there's no damn way I'll ever stop.

"Ella, when I say I'm going silent, that means I'm going silent. Do not call, text, email, send smoke signals, or whatever else. There's a reason we have two project managers, an estimator, and the rest of the guys. If you can't figure shit out, which is part of your job, maybe you should look elsewhere." It's too early for this. I've got a mom who doesn't question me this much. I'll be damned if someone I pay to work for me will act like she's my lord and keeper.

"Oh, well, okay." I walk away. She'll either get it or she won't; the ball is in her court whether she listens to me. Since her mouth was opening and closing, I'm thinking it's sinking in. I head to my office to get a few things out of the way, then make my rounds to the jobsites we've got going on, knowing in the next few weeks we're working on a restoration project where wood had rotted out the ass beneath the piled-on shingles through the years. It's going to be mammoth. Bringing in a few apprentices from the local high school who are taking construction classes will help. They won't be able to go on the roof to work, but they can harness in, watch the process, and help do the groundwork.

I take another sip of my coffee, look at the piles of papers on my desk, and wake my computer up, already jonsing to get out of the office. I need to hire someone else who enjoys paperwork, schmoozing people, and allows me to come and go more.

"Hey, you got a minute?" I glance up from my computer, happy something will distract me from this mess. I figured hiring a secretary would relieve a lot of the workload, and Ella did for the past seven years. This month and last, it's been a damn three-ringed circus. Changes are definitely brewing in the structuring of Sinclair Roofing.

"Chase, of course. What can I do for you?" I ask. My door is always open for employees to come in and talk to me about anything. Chase is one of my project managers, so if he asks to talk, I may need something a bit stronger than coffee.

"I've got an issue. Mind if I close the door?" Just as I assumed, something is wrong.

"Of course." I sit back in my chair, wondering if starting my own business was smart. Work is non-stop, there's zero down time, and taking half a fucking day off is backfiring on me big time today. Man, Mom would love to hear my thoughts right about now. She warned me to be prepared to work around the clock. She would know, since she's an entrepreneur herself in the form of an artist, painting canvases in an almost 3D-type portrait, except it's layered paint, which has made her successful, but with it came a lot of sleepless nights.

"I got a frantic phone call yesterday afternoon. Ella was losing her shit, saying something was wrong with you because you weren't returning her calls. I don't know what the hell is going on, but, man, I can't be at a jobsite and have that. Then she didn't even put the order in needed for next week's project, the Mockingbird House. We've got no damn wood ordered, let alone the other supplies." I run my hand down my face and close my eyes. A pulsing starts in my head. Next, my eye will start twitching, and then I won't be responsible for the words flying out of my mouth.

"And, Ledger, this isn't the first or the second time. I was able to pick up her slack the last few times. This one is going to bite us in the ass." Yep, gonna have to do something about Ella, and fast.

"Son of a bitch. You got the supply list. I'll go pick it up if I have to. We're not letting this slip through our fingers. We'd be fucked up the ass without any lube. Sinclair Roofing would be over, and we've all worked too fucking hard for that to happen," I tell him.

"You're not wrong. Hated to bring it up. I know Tulsa Rose is back in town and you've got your hands full. Figured you'd want to know before things go from bad to worse."

"I appreciate it, and yeah, I'm hoping to be around less, but that doesn't seem like it's going to happen. You ever want to step into more of a role here, I'd love to have you." I've tried to get him on board with being a partner. He's hesitant each and every time. The only other person I'd have ever offered that position to is Montgomery, even if he hated the roofing aspect; he was more of a man who wanted to work on a machine. Still sucks that he didn't have time to watch his dreams pan out. I rub the ache in my chest. It hits me all at once everything Mont is missing out on.

"Yeah, I hear you. Again. I'm not sure that I'd live up to the standards, though." Chase is younger, graduated from high school as I was really starting Sinclair Roofing, worked his ass off from the ground up, took the construction classes that I try to give back to, and hasn't left since.

"Are you kidding me? You'd surpass them. It's yours whenever. If you have the order sheet handy, I'll deal with it today. I need time away before I figure out what I'll be doing next." The need to go out to the front desk, tell Ella to pack her shit and leave indefinitely sounds like a mighty good idea.

"Let me think on it. Are we talking a pay raise?" I cock an

eyebrow at him. That question doesn't need an answer, but I'll give it to him anyways.

"If I had my way, I'd make you vice president, no buy-in necessary. We'd have a contract that would lock you in, and if you left, it'd be without getting a stake in the business. But yeah, you'd get a raise." Chase nods, hopefully evaluating more of the pros and less of the cons.

"Alright, I'll let you know soon. Meanwhile, here's the list. Good luck with Cruella de Vil out there." He stands up and places the paper on my desk. My eyes are already glancing down at the shit I'm going to have to load into my truck, meaning I'll be pulling a trailer. Not what I had in mind today when I came into work today.

"I see your niece has you watching movies again. More villains and fewer princesses?" His niece is with him every spare minute. His brother is a single dad, doing the best he can. Chase helps him out on the weekends unless work gets in the way.

"Yep, Sunny sure is. At least she's not making me wear tiaras, gloves, and carrying a wand with this kick she's on now. It sure will be nice if I can get her on a superhero kick. Sadly, four years in, and we're not there yet." He shakes his head. I stand as well, paperwork in one hand, phone in the other, coffee abandoned. This shit needs to get done. Fast.

"I hope Mack took pictures of that." We both laugh. Chase has no problem hanging with his niece, dressing up, having a tea party. Pictures being taken is where he draws the line.

"No fucking way. I'm out of here." He opens the door. I'm a few steps behind him. The issue with Ella can wait. Right now, I've got to fix these fuckups, make sure our customers are happy. After that, I'll figure out what the hell to do.

11

TULSA ROSE

My day was going so well. Too well. There were no tears. I was calm and tranquil while going through Mont's clothes. I needed a mental break from what I was working on; plus staying on one task is not my area of expertise. I like to jump around when it comes to cleaning, never sticking to one room. I'm like this in every aspect, especially work when I'm looking for a certain style of wallpaper and am unable to find it. I hop to something else if I get too stagnant in a search. So, I took the bags down the stairs one at a time and put them in the living room stacked around the couch to keep them separate from the trash pile in the foyer area since the outside garbage can was already over-flowing with trash—some from Mont's room, a lot from what I gathered up around the house. Ledger took care of a lot. The pantry was emptied out, and he kept the house well main-tained, as well as the pool, to name a few, but there were places in the house that needed a lot of attention, mainly drawers, hallway closets, and furniture where I found scraps of paper, a missing earring, bobby pins from that time I tried a new hairstyle in high school and needed to train my hair to go a certain way. It all piled up, making the house look like more of plastic facility than a home. I even put notes on what furniture pieces could be donated. The piano that no one played or learned how to use after Momma passed away should be put to good use, like a school or another family. She would have hated to see it sit stagnant. Daddy didn't touch a thing after Mom died, so lost in his grief that he clung to everything he could. Mont and I went through the majority, much like I'm doing now, minus furniture, heavy draperies that I'm bound and determined to take care of tomorrow, allowing the Florida sun to shine through the downstairs, paintings that need to come down, and walls that could use a fresh coat of paint. Then it'll be more to my liking. Less is more, which means the rugs in every room covering most of the hardwood floors will be either stored or donated. After taking a small break, I went back up to Mont's room to finish going through his dressers. Yes, two dressers. My brother liked his clothing. The nightstands were already done and now empty except for the remote to his television and his wallet. For some reason, it was hard to part with that—his license, debit card. Finding a picture of me and him together, worn from years of him keeping it tucked inside, hit me hard. If Montgomery hadn't come home after Mom passed away, I'm not sure how I would have survived. Dad was there in one capacity—to work. He was barely home to eat, leaving Mont to pick up the pieces, waking me up for school, making sure I ate a decent meal, and that I was thriving. His words always were, *Life is for the living.* Wisdom for a man who was thrust into becoming my very own hero. Which is why, when my hand reached around two envelopes, one addressed to me and one to Ledger, I was done for. Done in the way that my stomach sank to my feet. Done in the fact that the tears came so fast, they had me biting my fist in order not to have one of those gut-wrenching sob sessions I haven't had in years.

I grabbed my phone, needing Ledger in the worst way, only to remember he never gave me his new number last night. I could have asked. I *should* have asked, and probably would have if not for the wishy-washy emotions that ran through me after the bathroom scene yesterday. I could work around this. Besides, when the tough gets going, you get smart. I pulled up Sinclair Roofing through my internet browser, found his office number, clicked on it, and brought the phone up to my ear. It was that phone call that had me picking up the keys to my Tahoe, sliding on my flip-flops, and hitting the local watering hole. The call replays in my memory, confusing me even more.

"Sinclair Roofing, this is Ella, how can I help you?" I know that voice, remember the woman on the other end of the line, and it isn't in a good way.

"Hi, is Ledger available?" I don't give her my name or tell her the reason for the call; it's enough that I didn't hang up the second she answered.

"May I ask what this about?" Classic, answering a question with a question. I know it's a lost cause, but I make her aware that I'm back in town, and this time, I'm not leaving.

"Hi, Ella, this is Tulsa Rose. He was here last night, and I forgot to get his phone number. If you could pass along that I called, it would be greatly appreciated." I turned on my charm. Not for her sake; for mine.

"Will do." We both know she won't, the sneaky bitch that she is will keep the call to herself. What's a girl to do when the world is conspiring against her? Sit in her house and cry again? No thanks. I've done enough of that for two lifetimes.

"I can't believe my eyes. Tulsa Rose, are you home, sugar?" I plop down on an old barstool, the leather creaking in protest. I'm still in the cut-off jean shorts, tank top, hair piled on top, a piece of scrap fabric wrapped around my head to hold it back and away from my face.

"Hank, you're a sight for sore eyes, and yes, I am. I'm not leaving Orange Blossom unless it's to bring my best friend back or for work. I've sure missed you." A grandfather figure for a lot of us kids growing up, he'd keep an eye on me when I'd run the streets of the downtown area. The candy shop or ice cream place were where I'd be, then Hank would appear, standing outside the bar I'm now officially old enough to be in, watching over me while Montgomery took care of a few errands.

"Glad to see you home. Come here and give me a hug, then I'll buy your first round. Something tells me you need it." I'm out of my seat and flying around the bar, ducking under the old-fashioned opening that has the bar top on a hinge to open and close. Hank is wrapping me up in a bear hug I needed more than I realized. The smell of cigarette smoke, leather, and Old Spice envelops me.

"Oh, Hank, you may as well start a tab. It's been one of those days." He doesn't let me go, not even when I start to pull back thinking he'd be done with our hug. He squeezes me one last time, kisses the top of my head, and looks me over from head to toe in that fatherly way.

"Then you came to a good place. Tell me what you've been up to, what you want to drink, and if you're still eating pickles like they're popsicles." He moves toward the cash register. I don't leave behind the bar area yet, instead leaning on it to continue our talk.

"Vodka and cranberry, double, in a single glass, please."

Hank doesn't blink an eye. He must see how I feel on the inside. "As for pickles, the more the merrier. Do you still have the bacon cheeseburger on the menu?" I ask as he taps away on the cash register.

"We do. I suppose you want your usual with extra pickles and extra crispy fries?" Montgomery would stop by Hanks on a Friday night after work, have a beer or two, order our dinner, and bring it home. He never made me feel left out or that I was a nuisance, even though I knew there were times I was a total drag when it came to him coming and going. It wasn't until I got my license that he finally started hanging out with friends more regularly. Sadly, that's when he found the worst girlfriend ever.

"Yes." He sets my drink down in front of me not even two minutes later. The bar is dead at this time of day, and in the middle of the week no less. "I got a job at R&R, start next week. That's not the only reason I'm home, though. I missed this place. It took a long time for me to realize it, too dang long. A lot of therapy and a best friend who was willing to push me out of my comfort zone even if it meant she'd be staying back in Alabama."

"Glad you have that in a friend, sugar. Ledger still being an ornery old coot to you?" he asks. I laugh, spin around, and duck beneath the opening again to hide the blush on my face, also to compose myself in order to answer his question.

"Yes. You know he's done a lot, even if I didn't like a lot of what he did. Like Montgomery sending me away. I could have stayed here, done the same thing. I mean, I get it, but three more months, and I'd have graduated high school," I respond, getting back on my barstool.

"I've got a feeling there's more to the story than you

know. Mont wanted you home after college, no matter what. Seems our Tulsa Rose gained a backbone while she was away. He'd be proud of you, sugar." I swallow the lump that's lodged in my throat as well as a hearty sip of my drink, thankful he went heavy on the vodka.

"Maybe so. Now, I've got a question for you. Why is Ella Nixon working for Ledger, hmmm?" Hank shakes his head.

"You're going to have to ask Ledger that for yourself," is the response I get.

"He clearly doesn't know what she did to me while she was with Montgomery, or she'd have run from this town like the fires of hell were chasing after her." I sit back, my drink sucked dry. Hank is already refilling it for me. He's the absolute best.

12

LEDGER

"Who hurt you, sugar?" I hear Hank say as I walk into the bar. There, sitting in front of him, is Tulsa Rose. She doesn't know I'm there. I wouldn't doubt for a second that Hank realizes I'm standing off to the side of the now closed door. The man has a sixth sense, probably from being a bar owner since he landed back here after his time in the Vietnam War. Hank hasn't changed a bit, not that I've seen, since Montgomery and I started coming the minute he was back in town from college visiting and we were twenty-one. It's dark inside, windows smoked out to keep people from seeing in. The neon lights and the pool table lights are the only ones on. Same worn tables, chairs, and barstools. The only things Hank is diligent on is the bar, the kitchen, and the felt on the pool tables.

"Me. I hurt me. I fell in love with an asshole when I was sixteen years old. Then, when I was deep in my grief, thinking only about me, myself, and I, I dug a hole so deep, I'm not sure I'll ever be able to dig myself out." Tulsa doesn't say another word. Neither does Hank. I lean against the wall next to the door, shaking my head. It seems my butterfly has no damn idea. Her brother did, Hank does, and I damn sure knew the reason Montgomery had his will written the way it was for a reason.

"Well, sugar, pretty sure you're ahead of the game. You ready for a glass of water?" Hanks is already sliding one toward her.

"I'd prefer cranberry and vodka, but something tells me that won't happen unless I drink water. Way to ruin a woman's buzz." I barely hide my chuckle. She's smart, too smart not to see what was happening in front of her when she was too damn young, and my cock was too damn eager.

Hell, the reason I'm standing where I am today is for the woman in front of me. I busted my ass, paid a pretty penny for Ella's fuckup in terms of getting the supplies we needed in a timely manner. Driving from our town to the bigger city took half the damn day, but it was worth it to have every-thing on my truck and trailer. I took it straight to the jobsite, stored it in a packing container. I'm not fucking around with the weather raining on everything, or damn thieves. I've got enough trying to screw with this project already. Adding more would only piss me off further. As soon as that was dropped off, a quick stop at the office to unhook the trailer from my truck, and I was heading home. My phone didn't ring nearly as much as it did yesterday. Same went for the texts and emails. Maybe it finally settled in Ella's mind that I am not messing around. She has a job, should know how to do it. If she can't, well, there are more than enough people in town who are looking for a job. After a shower and a quick bite to eat, I headed straight to Tulsa's place. Seeing her truck was gone had me worried. It didn't stop me from using my key to let myself into her house for a quick look. I saw everything she accomplished in the hours I'd been at work. I was only there for a few minutes before I locked the door back, headed back to my truck, hopped in, and hit the road to find her. The first place I drove to, and there was her black Tahoe, parked up front and center. The rest of the parking lot was empty, since it's the middle of the afternoon. Hank's stays pretty quiet until the evening. Why he opens up at noon only to close when the crowd starts to thin out is anyone's guess.

"It's finished. Can I have another cranberry and vodka now?" Tulsa lifts the empty glass, the ice clinking around. The only other noise is the classic rock thrumming through the speakers. The televisions are showing a baseball game, but they're on mute.

"Yeah, sugar, you can have another, but it'll be your last." Hank gets to work on taking the empty glass away and concocting what I think has to be the bitterest drink you can order.

"That's not fair. You can take my keys," Tulsa Rose ponies up, tossing her keys on the bar top. "I'll stay in the back when I'm too tired, if you wouldn't mind taking me home whenever you close." I slowly walk toward them. Hank nods at me, garnering Tulsa's attention.

"Something tells me your ride is here, sugar. You want another drink, it's going to be up to Ledger, and I'm thinking he'd rather you don't puke in his truck," Hank tells her as I move behind her, my fingers dragging along her back.

"She can have another one. If she's anything like her brother, there won't be a mess, just a killer hangover the next morning," I tell Hank as I sit down beside her.

"I can order for myself. Hank, I love you. I'll have one

more. Ledger, don't annoy me and ruin my buzz." I watch as her tongue comes out and wraps around the small straw, pulling it into her mouth like she would my cock, a sight that will be happening very fucking soon.

"Love you, too, sugar, but even I know where my limit is. You're going to be hurting tomorrow, Tulsa." Hank hands her another drink. I give him the look. He gets it and knows she's cut off even if she doesn't think so.

"Butterfly, what has you drinking like a fish in the afternoon?" I ask, moving so I'm sitting sideways instead of facing straight ahead like Tulsa is. Another healthy sip, sucking back half the contents in her glass, has my eyebrows arching. It seems she's gearing up for battle, and knowing Tulsa, she'll be ready at dawn to fight anyone's demons, including her own.

"A lot of things. One, you know it's been seven years, seven years, and I still don't have your number? A girl needs that to apologize." Her pointer finger is up as she uses her other one to point at it. I start to say something. "Nope. Hush. This is my time. Two, why are you so nice and have such a... a... shit, I forgot what I was going to say." She's got both fingers up. The vodka is catching up to her, and it's about time I take her home. A yawn hits her, and she moves her hand to cover her mouth.

"Butterfly, mark my words, you can have my number and anything else you want of mine." I move in closer, telling her the words in a low voice so no one else can hear.

"Oh, okay." Yep, it's time to put the lightweight to bed. I'll be lucky if she makes it to the truck at this point.

"Hey, Hank, can you handle the Tahoe? I'm going to take Tulsa home. She's going to start fading fast, and I'm thinking it's going to be with her head on the bar top soon. Might be bad for business," I ask, taking my card out to pay her tab, not even getting a beer for myself.

"Yep, I'll have Max follow me to her place after closing. You know where the keys will be." Every year, Hank takes care of me when I let myself grieve the loss of my best friend, the feelings I have for his sister, the guilt that eats me up because of it. Soon, the day is going to come when I'll have Tulsa Rose as mine for good. There's nothing standing in my way anymore.

"Thanks." Hank takes the card even though I know he doesn't want to, especially when it comes to Tulsa Rose. He's got a soft spot for her that he rarely shows anyone. The Williams have a way of doing that, burrowing so deep without you even knowing it until they're firmly inside, never leaving.

"Not a problem. Sugar, it was good see you. Don't be a stranger now that you're home." He wraps his hand around hers, squeezing it lightly.

"I'm never leaving, Hank. Make sure you tell this one." She hooks her thumb in my direction.

"I think he's well aware, as are you. Now go take a nap, and not on my bar." I slide off my stool. Tulsa does the same, a little more unsteadily, making me wonder just how much she had to drink.

"Oh God, why is the room spinning?" She closes her eyes, one hand on the bar to hold herself up.

"Fuck it." I move, one hand going to her back, the other beneath the bend of her knees. Her arms wrap around my neck, and I'm walking to the door.

"Ledger, you feel like home," Tulsa mutters as I turn around, using my back to open the door. She moves further into the crook of my neck when the sunlight hits her face.

"Yeah, butterfly, you're my home, too." I only put her down in order to grab my keys out of my pocket, arm still banded around her lower back. The second the truck is unlocked, door open, I place her in the front seat and help her with the seatbelt, making sure she's secure. "Get some sleep, butterfly. I'll take care of you."

"Okay, wake me up when we get home." She turns toward me, tucks herself into ball, or as much as she can in the front seat of a truck, and closes her eyes. Tulsa Rose is going to be out like a light by the time I hit the road, and the only home she's going to is mine.

13

TULSA ROSE

I roll over, head pounding, cotton-mouthed, and ready to sleep the day away until I catch a whiff of the only man I've ever known to smell like the woods outside with a hint of leather. Ledger. That still doesn't have me popping out of the bed and scurrying away like any sane woman would do. What do I do instead? I roll over, grab his pillow, and bring it to my face, simultaneously smelling it while blocking the light out. Two birds, one stone. My hangover thanks me for it. Yesterday is coming back to me like a movie being rewound—the letter I found, calling Ledger's company and hearing a voice I loathe with every ounce of my being, then going to Hank's, where I ate and drank myself silly. Of course, Ledger would be the one to swoop in and save the day. It's not like in Alabama, where you can hire a car. That service doesn't run in Orange Blossom, and I am not complaining one bit. Our town is perfect the way it is, even if the town busybodies will be showing up at my doorstep any moment now.

"Butterfly, you stealing my pillow as well as my shirt

now?" Ledger's voice sounds muffled since the pillow is still pressed against my face. It's a sad day when you don't remember changing out of your clothes or climbing into bed with the man you've been lusting after for the better part of ten years.

"I'm keeping the shirt. Mont snatched the last one I stole. Speaking of, how'd I get into your clothes, and why am I in your bed instead of my own?" I ask, taking the pillow off my head, wincing. My damn head is trying to have a drum session without my permission.

"I'd like to say I'm surprised you stole my shirt, but since I left it there on purpose, I'm not. I should have known your brother would have seen through my ploy. And you're in my shirt because you walked your fine ass through my house, stripping along the way, saying you were hot. There's only so much a man can take, butterfly. I was at my wit's ends. It was either put you in my shirt or do something you wouldn't remember." I open one eye. He's hovering above me, hands on either side of my head, caging me in, shirtless and slick with sweat.

"Wait, what? You did that for me?" I ask but get no response. I grumble on with my annoyance and say, "Damn, I didn't even get an orgasm." I roll over, still processing the fact that I stripped for Ledger, and I'm in his shirt and in his bed. There's a playfulness in his tone, but there's also a hunger.

"Jesus Christ, Tulsa, I can only handle so much." If he only knew how that truly feels. Never have I been able to come unless it included Ledger in my fantasies. It makes for a real difficult time to get over the big jerk. "Are you givin' me the invitation, butterfly? Legs, thighs, ass, and it's perfectly on display for me." The tips of his fingers that weren't on my body a minute ago are now sliding along my ankles, going further. My legs are screaming in protest at the fact that I'm not widening them for his path, especially when he reaches the back of my knees. "I can smell you, butterfly. I know what I do to you. It's the same exact thing you do to me." I whimper in protest when he takes his fingers away. The man is a tease, and not in a good way.

"Ledger, I'm not sure how much more of an invitation someone can give you. If I were a weaker woman, I'd think it's me who's an issue, when clearly, that's not the case." I lose his warmth completely, figuring he's stepped back because God forbid Ledger takes anything further. The man is driving me freaking crazy.

"Get up, butterfly, and meet me in the kitchen. The first time I make you come with my fingers, it won't be with shit swirling through your head," he says close to my ear. I move my head to the side and see his green eyes shining brightly. Even the sun is doing its best to kick me while I'm down. He lifts his body away from me before I can respond, unprepared for the palm of his hand meeting my ass in a stinging slap. Which is absolutely not a turn-off at all. In fact, it has my core spasming, blood thrumming, and when his hand stays pressed against my skin, it has me pushing my hips, silently asking for more. "Tulsa," he groans, still holding the cheek of my ass in his hand. I feel the tips of his fingers dip deeper, almost grazing the fabric of my thong between each cheek. Never has he ever touched me the way he is now. Jesus, I need pickle juice for this raging headache, Nelle to talk me through the way Ledger switches from hot to cold, and last but not least, a pair of dry panties.

"Meet me downstairs. You've got five minutes, or I'm coming back up here, tossing you over my shoulder, and getting you downstairs myself. No fucking way we can talk about the shit we need to while you're tangled between my sheets in my bed, wearing my shirt." I let out the air I was unknowingly holding. My lungs are hurting, and the pounding in my head is only throbbing harder because of it. Fortunately, or not so fortunately, my bladder is wide awake, which means it's time to get out of Ledger's comfortable bed, brush my teeth, and deal with whatever he wants to talk about. Not that I don't have a lot to say to him either. Ugh, Ella? Really? How was he best friends with Montgomery and still hired that wretched snake? Don't get me wrong, she's pretty with her white porcelain skin, jet-black hair, and a confidence she carries really well, or at least she did back then. I'm willing to bet she still does. That doesn't make up for her personality and the snide remarks she'd make behind Mont's back when she was over. It took me months to finally tell my brother how rude his then girlfriend was. If he stayed with her or hooked up with her after—ick, by the way —I never knew about it. He protected me from as much as he could while no one was there to protect him from a drunk driver. God, life can be a tragic bitch.

I kick off the remainder of the sheets and comforter while still lying on my stomach, which doesn't help the epic hangover, while I roll over onto my back, groaning with each movement yet gearing up for what I'm going to say once I make my way downstairs. First, I've got to stand up, which makes for a humbling experience as my body decides to sway, tempting me to crawl back into bed, eat, breathe, and live there. I can tell you which drink will be added permanently to my list to never drink again: vodka and cranberry. My college years taught me *Jose Cuervo* is no friend of mine in the tequila department, and wine coolers. Maybe I should just mark off drinking from my list forever. The world stops spinning, my body quits rocking like I've been on a boat all day, and I gingerly walk to the bathroom, keeping the light off because there's no way I need to look in a mirror see myself, only to hide from the man who all of a sudden is ready for more than I think I'm prepared for.

"It's now or never, Tulsa Rose Williams. You wanted the answers, so don't be pissed when you don't get the right response," I tell myself after taking care of my morning necessities, albeit a little differently since I don't have a toothbrush here or a hairbrush. Probably better anyways not to run anything through my hair with my headache. I take one last deep breath, then head out of Ledger's room and down the stairs.

14

LEDGER

Sleeping next to Tulsa last night was not a hardship, even if I'm still struggling with blue balls. Hell, since the moment she rolled back into town, it's been this way, but last night, it was worse. All that beauty in my bed, wrapped around me, holding on to me with every slight movement. It didn't matter she was three sheets to the wind. Tulsa was practically on top of me the entire time. My hand and arm had nowhere to go, so I tucked my arm beneath her neck, hand on her outer thigh when she threw her leg over my waist. She may have gotten sleep, but I certainly didn't, having to recite purchase orders, think about the upcoming schedule, or revert to going over my football draft picks from last year.

"I really hope you have a jar of pickles or pickle juice in your fridge." Tulsa walks in, still in my shirt I tossed her last night once we got to my bedroom. No way was she staying home by herself last night. It didn't even cross my mind to drive her back to her place. Truthfully, Tulsa is right where she belongs.

"There're pickles. Not as many as what you have and probably not your favorite. Mom brought those over the last time we had dinner here." She opens the door. My white shirt on her body hides nothing with the light shining from the refrigerator, showing me her curves.

"Butterfly." I hiss out a breath. Thankfully, I'm sitting down, and it's a damn good thing, too, or I'd be right behind her, lifting the shirt that's already baring the bottom of her ass, an ass I just had my hands on not ten minutes ago.

"Oh, my goodness, your mother is a saint. She likes the good pickles." She lifts the jar to her mouth and takes a few sips from it, grimacing after each pull. Montgomery told me the way she eats pickles and has no problem drinking the juice after a long track meet to recover her muscles, she'd be a champ after a night of drinking when she went off to college. He wasn't wrong about that.

"The only saint in this room is me. How I've managed to keep my hands to myself is more than proof." Her back is to me, arched in a way a man wants her when he's taking her from behind, pulling on her hair while thrusting deep inside her wet heat. I take another sip of coffee, needing the caffeine to keep me awake. Tulsa slept from the early evening until only a bit ago. Since it's almost noon, I'd say she must have needed the sleep. I didn't think it was possible for someone to sleep damn near sixteen hours, yet she did. The last time I went up to check on her and saw she was awake, I knew it was time for us to have the talk we're about to have.

"Alright, did I just hear that correctly?" Tulsa turns around, jar of pickles still in one hand, the lid in the other, her curls twirling right along with her. The difference in yesterday's Tulsa and today's, she's more undone—her hair is down, and she's in a shapeless shirt, whereas when I picked her up from Hank's, it was the complete opposite. The tank is discarded in my bathroom, along with the tight-fitting jean shorts that cupped her ass like a glove. I much prefer the semi-naked state she was in my bed.

"You did. Get your pretty ass over here. We have shit to talk about." I scoot the barstool back, showing her where I'd like her to be.

"Nope, I'll stand right here." She takes another sip of the pickle juice before putting the jar on the counter, replacing the lid, and allowing the island to keep us separated. "Who's going first? Because I have a lot of questions, and I'm hoping I'll finally get the answers I deserve."

"Go ahead," I tell her, hoping like hell she remembers what she had on her mind last night.

"Okay, I'll broach the giant elephant in the room. Your phone number. I couldn't even apologize. I mean, seriously the shit I spewed at you wasn't okay." She starts pacing back in forth. Her headache must be dull if she's able move like she is now.

"It wasn't, but you were grieving. I never held a grudge against you. When that went down, it was a perfect storm. The company was changing shit around, and I knew you'd keep calling or texting." My phone rings on the counter. I ignore the noise since I told Chase I'd be out again today, not even bothering with calling the office to tell Ella. I'll only answer if it's important. The display on my phone tells me all I need to know.

"Huh, isn't that convenient. If the roles were reversed and my number wasn't working, what would you do?" she asks. My phone stops ringing only to start back up again.

"Ignore it. I am. The only important thing in my life is standing right in front of me."

"I'm finding that hard to believe, Ledger. You sent me away. I was too ashamed to call your mother, was ripped away from everyone I loved all because of a stupid piece of paper." She is getting pissed. My phone ringing continuously isn't helping matters either.

"Let me answer this to make sure the fucking office isn't burning down, and then I'm all yours." She nods and spins around, giving me her back, and moves back to the refrigerator to put the pickles away and probably help herself to whatever else to soak up the alcohol.

"This is Ledger," I answer the phone, annoyed because it's another instance where Tulsa has to wait on me. I hit the speakerphone button.

"Hi, Ledger, this is Ella. You usually stop by the office by now. I've sent you a few emails that need a response by this afternoon." The woman in front of me is staring me down, daggers in her eyes with every word Ella says over the phone line.

"I'll look at them now. If you need anything else, call Chase. I'm busy." The reason I'm about to slam my phone against the counter? Well, it seems Ella has hit a nerve with Tulsa. She's power walking out of the kitchen. I figure she's going upstairs to get away from Ella. I get it, really. No one is a fan of Ella, least of all Chase and I, but for Tulsa to stomp off? That's different.

"Oh, okay. Again?" she asks. I hear the side door slam shut.

"Yep. If you'd like to keep your job, I'd suggest you learn to cope without me at the office or answering you twenty-four hours a day, seven days a week." I hit the end button and throw my phone down on the counter. It seems I've got a wild butterfly on the loose.

I'm out the door, wearing nothing but my jeans, the top button undone. I still need a shower. Talking to Tulsa was the first thing on my mind. I follow her path, open the door, and walk around the side of the house to look for her. If it weren't for the fact that her wild hair is flying behind her, I may have missed her taking off down the trail that leads from my place to hers.

"Tulsa Rose, get your pretty ass back here! We can't talk if you run away from me," I tell her, picking up the pace. She has shorter legs than I do. For one of my strides, she needs to take two.

"Go away, Ledger! That cum-guzzling gutter slut can have your phone number, work for you, yet you couldn't fit it in your time to respond. Shit, the *Return to sender* on the letter I sent should have been an answer enough. No answer is an answer. Damn, you could have at least said, *Lick it, put a stamp on it, and mail it to someone who gives a shit!*" She doesn't stop run-walking until I make it to her, hands going to her hips, my front against her back. I'm stunned speechless. I have no idea what the hell she's talking about.

"I give a damn. I'm not sure what happened, where our lines were crossed, but I'm going to give this to you straight. I was protecting you, in a weird fucked-up way, giving you time to spread your wings, not to keep you at arm's length. I gave Flay my number. If you had called him, he'd have given it to you without hesitating. As for Ella, we'll discuss that, and soon, but right now, we've got our own issues before adding others into the mix." My hands that were gripping her hips wrap around her lower waist, my lips at her ear, but that still doesn't calm her down.

"Well, Ledger, I should have done a lot of things. We both should have." I can feel how tense her body is. The emotion swirling through her body are not grief; its hurt with a tinge of anger.

"You're right. Will you come back inside? My work knows I'm off for the day. Now,"—my nose nudges her hair away from her neck, my mouth salivating at that thought of grazing my tongue along her skin, finally getting a taste of her—"it's hot out today. Our feet are liable to catch on fire, and I'd rather not get sunburnt." Unable to control myself, not that I ever could around the woman in my arms, I graze my lips along her neck. A sweep of my tongue glides along her pulse point. Her body melts, the tension is gone, and in its place is the Tulsa I know and love.

"Fine, but I can't be held responsible if you keep touching me like you are. You've kept my body on a slow sizzle, and I'm damn tired of holding out," she admits.

"Tulsa, we're going to happen. I'm telling you right here and now, soon the whole fucking town will know that you're mine. You want to know why your brother put that stipulation in his will? It's because he knew. He saw the hunger in my eyes, saw the way you twitched your ass around me. And the shirt he stole? It was all on purpose. I don't fault him for it. You shouldn't either. He was protecting you. We're the ones who screwed up along the way." I back away from her. My hand reaches for hers, and I lock our fingers together.

"You're right. We have a lot to talk about. I get where he was coming from even if I don't like it. Let's go back to your place. My hangover is finally leaving, and I'm suddenly starving." My butterfly turns, and I see can her light brown eyes, the combination of brown, gold, and green.

"If this is your way of getting me to make waffles and bacon, all you had to do was ask."

"Fine, will you please make me breakfast?" Her head is tipped up. My own dips down. I'm still holding her hand, so my other moves to her lower back, bringing her closer to me. Then I take her mouth with mine. My first taste of many. When I told her she was my home, I wasn't kidding. Her soft plush lips move beneath mine, and a low moan leaves her, allowing me the entrance I was going to get regardless of the outcome. Her tongue wraps around mine, and the moment her warm hand presses against my lower stomach, fingernails pressing in, I know I'm a fucking goner. My hand moves, gripping the fabric, pulling it up until it's out of my way and my hand is cupping the cheek of her ass. My cock wakes up, stirring in the confines of the denim, becoming harder, thicker, ready to be inside her.

"Butterfly." I pull back to gather myself, attempting to gain composure before I'm ripping her shirt off, backing her up until she's against a tree, I'm ripping open my jeans, and am finally getting inside the only woman I've ever fucking wanted. "Let's take this to the house, okay?" Tulsa nods in response. I step back. Her eyes are a blazing inferno, tongue coming out to lick her lips as her eyes lock on my torso then glide down to my cock. There's no hiding it, not that I will. Not now and not ever again. Tulsa is no longer the teenage girl. I'm still ten years older, but at least this time around, she's more than legal.

15

TULSA ROSE

"You know Ella and Montgomery dated when I was sixteen, right? I walked in the house one day after school, and she was in the kitchen, baking cookies like she was married to Mont," I tell Ledger as he pours the batter into the waffle iron. The bacon is sizzling on the griddle.

"I'm aware." He looks up from what he's doing.

"What I didn't tell you is that she was naked minus one of Mom's aprons." I internally gag, maybe throw up in my mouth a little bit, which sucks because after the kiss Ledger laid on me, I don't want to think of Ella in the same sentence.

"Fuck, that's not cool." He shakes his head, a disgruntled look on his face.

"Oh, that's not all. Some of it was my fault. I didn't tell anyone, thinking Mont really liked this girl or loved her even. So, I took all the snide remarks, her talking about how I'd never grow into my body, how braces weren't attractive to boys, and how they wouldn't kiss a girl while I had them." I roll my eyes. As if I was looking at any boys in high school. My sights were set on Ledger. There was never anyone else. "One day, Montgomery walked into the house, heard Ella make one of her remarks about me living off my brother and that I would never amount to anything if it weren't for him. That's when he ended things. He kicked her out. She was crying and screaming. It was kind of pathetic. I guess it wasn't really over like I thought, since she's working for you. I assume there was something between them because if Montgomery told you any of this, I know she wouldn't be at Sinclair Roofing." Ledger wanted to talk. This was easier than the fact I'm sitting on two letters in Mont's bedroom at our house or the slew of other things we've yet to unfold.

"The only reason she has a job at Sinclair Roofing has to do with Montgomery. She came to my office shortly after you left claiming to be pregnant. I had no idea about her being a cunt to you. I should have, though. Chase brought it to my attention three months later that she wasn't showing. I asked her about it, so caught up in my own grief. Mont was gone, you were gone, and I was burying myself in work, drowning out life. Ella stated she had a miscarriage. That's an area I've got no expertise in. I left it at that. She did her job, stayed away from me. Things were fine. Now they aren't. She's becoming a pain in my ass. I'm about to set her ass loose. The unemployment line is calling Ella's name." A deep gasp escapes me. If she was pregnant and lost the baby, that means she lost a piece of my brother, my mother, and our father. I'd have lost years with my niece or nephew. I shouldn't think about myself, especially after holding my best friend as she had to have a D&C when her body rejected her baby.

"Do you think... Oh God, you don't think that it was a lie,

or she got rid of the baby, do you?" The hunger I once had for breakfast is fading quickly.

"The truth? I don't think she was pregnant at all. Your brother only hooked up with her a time or two that I can recall after the two split up. Don't really see him not wrapping it up either. He was only getting started in his career. His sole focus was on his land clearing company outside of you." I let out a sigh of relief even though she played Ledger dirtier than dirty.

"Well, judging by the mega box of condoms I found in Mont's room, I think you're right." Major ick. I mean, sex is normal, but thinking about your brother in the same sentence, no thanks. "That's so gross, if that's the truth. Ella should be ashamed of herself." The bitch doesn't deserve the good fortune of a job at Sinclair Roofing, let alone the gum on the bottom of someone's shoe.

"I'd agree with you there. Put your number in my phone and call your line." He places his phone on the counter in front of me.

"Password?" I ask, feeling like I've hit pay dirt on one of those gold mining shows. Seven years later, and we're finally getting to the place we should have been all along. God, I'm an idiot. I really need to set up an appointment with my therapist to make sure I'm navigating this relationship in a healthy manner.

"Ten-twenty-nine, butterfly, the same it's always been." My mouth drops open, hangs there for a moment. "Close your mouth, Tulsa Rose, or you'll catch flies," Ledger tells me as he sets a heaping pile of waffles, bacon, and jar of peanut butter in front of me, along with a glass of sweet tea. He knows my preference of drinks in the morning. I'd try to drink coffee here or there growing up. Even through college,

I tried the liquid sludge but preferred the taste of the ice cold drink instead. Hot tea was much the same. Now, sweet tea I can definitely drink, which means it's my caffeine of choice first thing in the morning.

"This looks great. Do you think after we eat and you take care of things you need to here, we can head to my house? My time is dwindling down, and I'd like to get through a few more rooms before starting work." He deserves to have the letter Montgomery left him, and truthfully, I'd really appreciate him being in the same room when I read the note my brother left me.

"Yep, I've got no plans. The Tahoe should be there, too. I asked Hank to drop it off when he closed the bar. While you're doing your thing, I'll load up the donations you've got piled everywhere. I take it you couldn't wait for me to help you carry them down the stairs?" He stuffs his mouth with a piece of bacon. I'm still slathering the peanut butter on a waffle, then pouring the syrup until there's a thin coat on the top. My food choices are weird to some, but they work, and I like the flavorful combination each bite gives you.

"Nope, it had to be done. I can't expect you to drop what you're doing at work to carry a few boxes upstairs or lug trash bags down the stairs, which honestly, I dragged them down, so it's not like it was hard work." I shrug my shoulders and cut into the waffle, ready to take my first bite of Ledger's legendary waffles.

"You've got my number. Use it. Nothing is more important than you. Finish eating. I'm going to hop in the shower, get changed, and then we'll head to your place." I nod, my own mouth full of food. He walks around the island, muscular chest flexing and pulling with each step he takes. My eyes are soaking him up. "Christ, I want to take your mouth, butterfly, but if I do, there'll be no stopping. We'll both be naked, and there's something in your eyes that tells me we've got more to deal with." His nose slides along mine. "Be back soon. Eat up. You're going to need it." I swallow. Ledger is right about a lot of things. He's also left my core clenching, nipples pebbled, and has me wanting to follow him up the stairs.

16

LEDGER

"So, um, while cleaning out Montgomery's things yesterday, I found something. Actually two some-things." While I was in the shower, Tulsa finished eating, cleaned up the kitchen, and found her flip-flops by the front door. What she didn't do was walk upstairs to join me in the shower. We loaded up in my truck, drove over here so I could help her pack the trash into the back for us to drop it off later today.

"More than the box of condoms you mentioned?" I'm going through a pile she set aside while sitting on Mont's bed when she comes to sit beside me after she cleaned herself up. Her wet hair is falling down to her waist, and she's in another tank, an oversized zip up hoodie on top, and a pair of shorts.

"Ick. I still can't think about that, but yeah. I found these." I drop the football I was holding in my hand, the one he kept from our football playing days. A lump forms in the back of my throat, and I'm unable to speak a single word. No wonder she tied one on last night then slept an ungodly amount. This has been sitting heavily on her mind the entire time. "I know my brother, always prepared for the worst, anal in his organization of any and all paperwork. Yesterday, I wasn't prepared to open my letter. Today, it seems a little bit easier." My hand goes to hers. I'm still at a loss for words, need her touch to settle the ache building in my chest that her brother, my best friend, would go to the trouble of leaving us each a note. And what are the odds we're finding them ten years later?

"Yeah." My response comes in the form of a croak. Why wouldn't he leave these with Flay? Damn Montgomery for this. Just when a door closes on losing him, another is flung wide open.

"Do you, um, want some time alone to digest this?" Christ, she should still hate me for pushing her away, inadvertently keeping her away from her home for far longer than I ever thought she would. That's a lie. I knew her stubbornness the moment she made that call telling me the words that sliced my heart open, aware of the fact she was angry, hurt, upset. Experiencing so much tragedy in her young life will do that to a person. Clearly, things have changed between us, for the better.

"No, butterfly, I'd prefer you here." I lie back. Tulsa moves with me. My arm wraps around her shoulder, tucking her in closer to me. The letters she is holding are now on my chest, lying beneath her hand, damn near on my heart. "Give me a minute. We'll read them together?"

"Yeah, that might be better than doing it alone." She tips her head up toward mine. My lips graze hers, needing her like I never have before. At a small nip of her bottom lip, a sigh leaves her, allowing me to deepen the kiss. My tongue slides inside, and hers wraps around mine. Anytime I'm with her like this, everything else fades away. I need more. I maneuver us until she's flat on her back. My hands cup her cheeks, not wanting to lose this moment where I finally have Tulsa beneath me, my mouth consuming hers. The noise that swirls inside my head quiets. There's no work, no letter to think about, and Tulsa doesn't hate me for pushing her away, trying to do the right thing not only for herself but also because it's what Montgomery would have wanted. There's none of that. It's her hands on my lower stomach, beneath my shirt, moving dangerously close to the edge of my jeans. My hand moves slowly down the length of her body until I reach her leg and hitch it over my hip, causing my body to sink into hers further, my cock pressing into her center. Soon, really fucking soon, there won't be a damn thing in between us. The tips of her fingers slide lower. "Butterfly, you keep touching me like that, and you're going to get more than you're ready for." I pull away. We're both trying to catch our breath. Her eyes are hooded, lips wet from our kiss, and her cheeks are flush with color.

"Ledger, it's you who needs to realize that I'm ready. I have been long before I came home to Orange Blossom." She brings her other leg up and hooks her ankles around one another, pressing her center against my cock yet again. I'm not sure how much longer I can hold back.

"Fuck, you're making it hard for me to be a gentleman. One thing's for sure. When I take you, it won't be in your brother's bed." Her nose scrunches up, she drops her legs, and the desire that was thrumming through her body slowly fizzles out.

"Ick. Way to be a lady boner killer, Ledger Sinclair." She makes the noise to go along with the word. "Probably good we stopped anyways. We need to read these letters, or at least I need to. It's the final door of closure that I had no idea was necessary for me, one final piece of my brother."

"You're right. Let's do this." I stand up, hand going out to help her sit up.

"Okay, here's your letter. We'll read them together but not aloud. I'm not sure I can handle doing that without crying." She hands me the letter addressed to me.

My hand trembles as I see my name written in Montgomery's signature scrawl. I settle down on the floor, back meeting the dresser. Tulsa moves so she's sitting across from me, our legs touching one another's once we straighten them out.

"You good?" I ask while I slide my finger beneath the sealed envelope, preparing myself for the unknown.

"I am. Strangely enough, it's bringing me a sense of peace." With that settled, I pull the letter from the envelope, take a deep breath, and settle in.

Ledger,

If you're reading this, it means I'm long gone, living on the other side, watching down on you and Tulsa Rose. I know, you know. Not that it wasn't obvious to see, the looks, the way you handled her by not going after something you couldn't have. It means more than you'll ever know. Tulsa is one of a kind, stubborn like only the Williams are, and goes after what she wants, no matter who's standing in her way. Which is why, without a doubt in my mind, you went along with what I left in the will. I know it's going to hurt, not only her but you as well. Thank you. Thank you for being there for all of us.

Take care of yourself, take care of my sister, keep her safe, and love her like I know only you can. Life is for the living. Until we meet again, brother.

Love,

Montgomery

I close my eyes and tip my head back. The letter floats to my lap. I'm too busy trying to keep my emotions in check, trying my damn hardest not to break down, to be strong, for myself, for Tulsa, and damn it all to hell, for Mont. Fuck, I could kick his ass, making us wait all these years later, only for Tulsa to find them when it could have been as simple as leaving them with Flay. Fucking drama llama. A chuckle escapes me because this is exactly who he is, and damn does it make me miss him even more.

17

TULSA ROSE

My eyes leak like a fountain as I read the words in the letter, watching as every tear transfers onto the paper, smearing the ink and ruining the most priceless thing I have to my name.

Tulsa Rose,

Where do I begin? I guess the hard stuff needs to come first. I've written this letter and rewritten it a thousand times over. The fact that you're reading this means I've failed you, that I left you after everyone else did, too. I'm so fucking sorry. If it's any consolation, I was hoping to destroy this by the time you were off to college. No luck there. Don't hate Ledger for sending you away. I saw the way you were around him, too close to being of legal age that I couldn't keep the two of you apart. Not my main *goal anyways. You are destined for big things, and if you stayed in Orange Blossom for college, you'd never experience the best part of your twenties life has to give.*

I suck back some of my tears, knowing he lost out on his experience when Mom passed away. And when Daddy was gone, too, Montgomery definitely wouldn't leave. Instead, he took business classes online, only in the beginning stages of getting his own business up and off the ground for a drunk driver to destroy his dreams, making him leave this earth entirely too soon.

I'm sorry that I won't be at your graduation, either of them, or to watch you marry my best friend, because it's not an if, it's a when. I have one word of advice. It's to live like today is your last, love with your whole heart, and to never take advantage of tomorrow. Tomorrow may not come. Anytime you need to talk, I'll be in the woods across from the pond.
Love you big, baby sis,
Montgomery

The gaping hole in my heart that was only starting to scab over bursts wide open. I hold the letter to my chest, bring my knees in closer, and wrap myself up in a ball. No one prepares you for a handwritten letter, the one you can visualize your brother writing while sitting at the kitchen table or on the back patio, where he hung out when he needed to calm himself down from work, from me being an annoying sister, or because life was not kind to the Williams kids, even more so for Mont. It didn't bother him, or at least he didn't show it. My big brother, the man who put everything on the line, didn't once think about himself when Mom passed, took care of me in a way Daddy no longer could, believes he failed me, and now I can't tell him that he did everything imaginable. I'm so distraught, swallowed up by my own feelings, unaware of the presence surrounding me. His big body somehow manages to wrap around me, filling me with a warmth I had no idea I needed. The sobs wreck my world, and I feel like I'm back to square freaking one.

"Get it out, butterfly, get it out." Ledger holds me closer, allowing me the time I need to cry. I realize I've yet to make an appointment with my therapist or talk to Nelle about what's been going on, thinking I can just wade right in and not feel any blowback. The crumpling of the letter has me slowing down my tears. Plus, who really wants to ugly cry in front of the man who has owned your heart for as long as you can remember? Not me.

"Why does it hurt so much?" I lift my head, asking the question, trying to breathe through the pain that is consuming me.

"He doesn't want you to hurt, butterfly, I promise you that." He slides the letter away from my chest and tosses it on top of his. Montgomery didn't write this long elaborate four-page letter, thank God, or I'd have never gotten through the whole thing.

"Montgomery." I deep breathe. A hiccup comes out, and that's when I realize it's time to do my exercises my therapist taught me—inhaling, holding it in, counting the seconds, closing my eyes, and going to my happy place. One where I was a child, my family wasn't gone, and I could run around the orange groves up and down the street across from our house, barefoot and wild through each row, hands out, touching the leaves on the trees, smelling the sweet citrus, coming home sticky from eating one too many oranges. Now, the orange groves are abandoned, there are no sprinklers on when a Florida drought hits us in the dead of summer, and all that's left is blossoms every now and then. The fruit, though, it's long gone

"Oh God, Ledger, he said that he failed me. How could he ever think that? Mont took care of everyone and everything, so selfless. He could never have failed me. The drunk driver did that, taking him away when he barely was able to explore life, to find a love like our parents shared, one that consumed them in the best possible way, taking Daddy right along with Momma. He'll never experience half of what he deserves." Life is precious. Life is also really fucking unfair. Ledger grabs my hips and pulls me closer so my thighs are on top of his. Nothing about this is sexual. This is Ledger being Ledger, taking care of me. No wonder he and Montgomery were best friends.

"Tulsa Rose, his biggest joy was you. Don't drown in one word out of I'm sure the many he wrote. If he were here right now, he'd be kicking both of our asses, telling us to do the shit he couldn't, don't you think?" One of his hands moves from my hip to cup my cheek, tipping my head from its downward position to look at his eyes. I notice this beautiful man before me has redness around his own. Clearly, this is eating him up, too.

"You're right. That damn saying of his, *Life is for living.*" I roll my eyes. Montgomery took life by the horns, bull or no bull.

"That sounds about right. I think we're done in Mont's room for the day. Let's go grab some food, veg on the couch, and call the donation center to get some of the piles cleared up, alright?" He doesn't get up first. He holds me there, head lowering and whispering his lips against mine, giving me exactly what I need.

"I'd love that. Can we eat on the back patio? I cleaned it off earlier today. I'm afraid there's no room on the couch for us to sit." I shrug my shoulders. My brother was a shoe whore—boots, sneakers, boat shoes, he had them in spades. And don't get me started on the graphic tees. I kept the ones that were his favorites. I've got an idea for them.

"Sure, I'll order dinner, unless you went shopping for more food besides sandwich fixings."

"Uh, I did in fact not make it to the grocery store. Hank's is one thing. Going to the grocery store before stopping at your mom's, apologizing, and saying hello is another thing entirely." Ledger smirks, knowing exactly how his mom can be.

"Smart move. Then it's settled. Figure out what you want to eat, and I'll get it ordered." I spin my body, watching my legs in order not to kick him in the stomach, and start to make my way off his lap. He doesn't let me, though; he's got both his hands around my middle, holding me to him. This time, I know it's more for him and less for me, so I stay exactly where I am because that's where Ledger needs me to be.

18

LEDGER

"I think you might be too big for my bed, Ledger," Tulsa Rose says as we're lying in her bed next to one another. We ate dinner of turkey BLTs, neither of us wanting to ride into town when she had everything in the house from my grocery trip the other day. It didn't take long with the two of us working beside one another, Tulsa slathering the bread with mayonnaise, slicing the tomatoes and lettuce, throwing the turkey on, then assembling the bacon on top after I fried it up. She scarfed down her sandwich along with half a jar of pickles, this brand filled with dill and garlic, enough that she could chase a vampire away. It still didn't stop me from kissing her. We had a few beers, turned on the outdoor television. She looked longingly at the pool, which reminded me I need to get it taken care of soon. The days are only getting hotter, which means I'll be the lucky son of a bitch to feast my eyes on Tulsa in a bikini.

"You're right, but it's not going to stop me from sleeping next to you. Hell, the last time, you slept on top of me." I'm in my boxer briefs. She's in my shirt she found in the bottom of Montgomery's closet and a pair of panties. It seems she likes my clothes more than her own, which is more than fine with me. She looks better in them than I do. Plus, I get the perks of an easy access, to hold on to her, skin on fucking skin.

"Don't act like it's a hardship." She hitches her leg over my hip. My hand slides down her back to the end of her shirt, bunching up the fabric so I can get my hands on her body.

"Not at fucking all. Though next time, we're at my place." Her cold foot hits the inside of my legs, causing me to hiss out a breath. Not like I've got much room to move anywhere else. We're in a queen-size bed. My six-foot-plus frame is a joke. Another inch or two, and I'd be hanging off the mattress.

"Hmmm, I don't know. I've had an awful lot of fantasies with you here in my bedroom and in this very bed." She wiggles closer to me, the seam of her pussy against my body. My hand wanders further down the length of hers.

"Where's your head at, butterfly?" I ask. If we're going to dig into the two of us, I want to make sure she won't have any damn regrets. She's been quiet. Nothing like the catatonic state one would be after all the shit she's been through. More like she's in her own head, trying to pick every puzzle piece apart.

"I'd be a lot better if you'd quit holding back." My cock can only take so much, and I'm about at my wit's end with doing what she's accused me of, but first, I need to make sure she understands what's happening between us.

"Don't evade my question, and then we'll talk about exactly what you did in this room while thinking about me."

I groan as her hand slides along my abdomen, fingertips soft, delicate, and all Tulsa Rose.

"I'm okay. While it opened a wound, it also healed a big part of my heart. Thank you for reading your letter beside me." After we got up from the floor, we talked about what Mont had to say. She didn't need the words; it's been a long time coming. Tulsa Rose has been mine since the moment she hit six-fucking-teen. There wasn't a boy or man in Orange Blossom who wasn't aware of it. Same went for Alabama. The weekends I was there, any fucker who was sniffing around her was run off with one look. Seeing a six-foot-plus, solid two-hundred-and-thirty-pound man will do that to the little city boys who work out in their air-conditioned gym.

"There's nowhere else I'd rather be. Now that I know your head is clear, I'm going to tell you how this is going to go. We lost ten years to our foolish pride. You're twenty-seven; I'm thirty-seven. We're not going another ten years where you're somewhere without me. You understand the reason behind why Mont wanted me to do what I did. It ripped my heart out of my chest to push you away, but I'd do it again, and I know that pisses you off. You, Tulsa Rose, deserved to chase after your dreams, then, after you conquered the world, come home to me and Orange Blossom. You're home now. We've got a lot of time to make up for. Maybe you understand, maybe you don't, butterfly, so I'm going to lay it out plain and fucking simple. I'm staking my claim. Forever."

"I'm glad you and Montgomery knew what I wanted, which was being with you in whatever capacity I could have you. If you ever try to send me away again for this hero bull-shit, I will knee you in the balls so hard, kids will be an issue, and that'd be a damn shame because I want at least four. That being said, you deserve to know that I'm sorry for being so mean, and by doing so, I want you to read the letter I wrote. I understand you didn't want anything to do with me. I was a complete bitch." The light is still lit on her side of the bed. Tulsa rolls over, getting out of the bed while giving me a view of her ass. The preference of her wearing a tiny thong does nothing to stop the ache in my cock. She may not know it, but I'm going to get a taste of her tonight.

"I never got a letter. Not sure what happened, but I assure you I would have at least read it." I move to sit up, my back against the headboard as she bends over, digging through a box. I don't give a fuck about a letter. We both made mistakes, but it's over and done with. A fresh start is all that matters to me, but if this is what she needs, this is what she'll get.

"Aha! There it is, the little booger." I laugh at her antics. One thing about Tulsa, if it means something to her, she's going to keep it forever. It doesn't matter what it is—a movie stub, a letter, a ring you made out of a gum wrapper, she'll display it proudly too. "Here you go." She climbs onto my lap, straddling me, notching her pussy right on my cock. The little hellion knows exactly what she's doing. I lift my hips, letting her feel what she continuously does to me.

"I'll read your letter later. I've got you right where I want you. Fuck the rest of it." My hand goes to the back of her neck, moving her down. Her eyes flutter closed, nipples puckered beneath the cotton shirt.

"Ledger, you're making it really hard to concentrate." She thrusts the letter between us. My gaze locks on the *Return to sender* written on the outside of the envelope. I'm seeing Goddamn red. It's hard not to recognize it. I take it out of her hand, turn it over, examining and noticing that the seal has been tampered with. "Did you open this when it came back to you?"

"No, I put it away with my pile of cards and things Nelle has given me through the years." Probably in a shoe box at that top of her closet, if I'd hazard a guess.

"That fucking cunt," I breathe out, fire burning through my veins. This is it. That bitch is going to be blackballed in the whole damn county. "A liar, a damn thief, which this is a damn big issue right here." I hold the note up, waving it in the air, still not caring what she wrote inside. "Messing up on purchase orders, not doing her job. Well, Ella has screwed up one too many times. First thing tomorrow morning, she'll be out on her ass."

"I'd like to say I'm sad about the situation. It's not even the letter that upsets me; it's how she played you, bringing Montgomery into it, a low no one should ever stoop to, and for whatever reason, because you know there's one." Son of a bitch. Tulsa Rose is right. Ella's after something. What the cause is I've got no clue. The worry is what she was hoping for long term. The date on that letter is less than a month after Ella came to work for my roofing company.

"Christ, shit just keeps getting deeper and deeper. I'm about ready for a damn vacation, and work is busier than ever," I tell her.

"Don't look at me. I'm nowhere near vacation time. New job, remember?" That means I've got the weekend with her after I deal with this situation.

"Then I guess it's time to finally get a taste." I lick my lips. She sweeps her center along my cock, and that's all the confirmation I need.

19

TULSA ROSE

"See? That doesn't work for me. It's not fair that I'll be on orgasm number two while you've yet to receive one." I'm on his lap, hands reaching for the edge of his tee I'm wearing, pulling the fabric up higher. I'm wearing nothing beneath, unveiling myself to Ledger one inch at a time. The flex of his length against my core tells me he likes that idea.

"Butterfly, you want that, you better spin your sexy self around, back that ass up until you're sitting on my face and my cock is your mouth." My eyes lower, landing on his chest, the thick wall of muscles turning me on further. "Fuck, you like that. Come on, Tulsa Rose, give us both what we want."

His words make me move, fingers sliding beneath the band of his boxers. Ledger lifts his hips while I scoot back, taking the fabric with me, getting my first glimpse at his thick shaft. "Holy shit, you're huge." A chuckle whispers across the room. I abandon taking off his shorts and lower my head, hand grasping his cock, feeling the soft velvet skin beneath my palm.

"Son of a bitch, you keep that up, I'm not going to last. Been dreaming about having that sweet mouth of yours wrapped around my cock," Ledger grunts when I lap at the drop of precum. I moan at the taste. It's salty yet sweet. I lift my head back up and resume my journey, realizing I'm the one who is going to make him lose his mind if I take too long.

"What else have you dreamt about, Ledger?" The shorts are off his body. He slides down on my bed, feet hanging over the edge, and stands up for a moment, tossing his boxer briefs on the ground.

"Sit on my face. I'll use my tongue to describe with every letter all the things I've done to you in this very room while I jacked my cock. Shit, butterfly, I should be arrested for some of my thoughts." He holds his hand out for me to take, guiding me as I lift one leg over his lap, his hands cupping the cheeks of my ass, spreading them. "Look how wet you are for me, butterfly." I drop to my elbows. A finger slides along the seam of my slit. My core clenches, grasping at something to hold on to. Ledger moves his hands until they're wrapped around my thighs and pulls me back until I can feel the plume of air from his breath following his finger.

"Ledger." I arch my spine, situating myself to where I can work my mouth along his cock.

"Yep, gonna lick this pretty pussy while you suck my cock. The only question is, who's going to get there first?" His tongue licks me from clit to ass. I hum in rapture. Wanting him to experience a similar feeling, I work my mouth over the tip of his dick, relishing in the way he sucks in a breath. We're stomach to stomach. There's no denying how each of us feels. My thighs widen as I settle on his face further. His hips arch up to push his cock further inside my mouth. I oblige, unable to stop from finally having Ledger beneath me. Even if he's trying to kill me, it puts a whole new perspective to death by tongue.

"Oh God." I pull away from barely taking two or three inches of his cock inside my mouth. Ledger choses that moment to use his teeth along my clit. A quiver takes over the entirety of my being. He flattens his tongue to soothe the delicious onslaught of sensations rolling through me. It makes me go back to his cock, using my forearm to hold me up, my other hand holding the base of his shaft, twisting my palm since there's no way I'll be able to take his full length. He's that long and that thick. I find my groove, luxuriating in the way he seems to be stumbling with his ministrations along my center. His thumb is inside my center, lips wrapped around my clit. He's going to try and make me orgasm before I'm ready. Not that I'm complaining, but it would be freaking awesome if I could make him come first, feel the pleasure rock through his body firm in the knowledge that I, Tulsa Rose Williams, can make Ledger Sinclair weak in the knees first. When I finally get the hang of things, my jaw slackens more, and I relax the muscles in my throat and move my hand off his cock. This time taking him deeper, further, until my gag reflex causes me to pull back, only to redouble my efforts again and again. Ledger must know what I'm up to, since he takes his thumb out of my pussy, one hand pressing down on my lower back, causing me to arch my spine even more. Two fingers move in a back-and-forth motion inside of my wet depths while his thumb presses against that forbidden bundle of nerves, heightening the way I'm experiencing my first time with him. And let me tell you, he does not disappoint. No amount of toys or fingers can compare to the real-life action happening between my spread thighs.

"Fuck," he moans against my core as I take the whole of his length to the back of my throat, finally without gagging. I swallow around him, and he presses his thumb deeper, sucking harder, and moving his fingers faster. It has me keeping my head firmly down, breathing through my nose to stay there, worried that if I pull off him, I won't be able to get this far down again.

"Goddamn, butterfly, if you don't want to swallow my cum, I suggest you move now." His mouth leaves my pussy, his fingers still creating all that magic, thumb now up to his first knuckle. Never in my life did I think this experience would be this freaking amazing. It makes me want to take more than just his thumb, to maybe know what it would feel like to have his cock inside me while either my fingers or his are buried between my soft thighs, or even a toy. Now, that's an idea I should definitely bring up to him.

"Hmm," I moan around his length, not letting up. He lifts his hips, thrusting into my mouth and somehow managing me to take him deeper. His body locks up tight, the ministrations on my body stop, and the first jet of his cum hits the back of my throat.

"Swallow for me. Show me how much you like the taste of me," he groans. I do as he demands. He gave me an out earlier, allowing me the choice on whether to back off or not. I'm not a quitter or a spitter, so with each spurt that leaves his body, I suck it down, greedily taking it all, not stopping until his body relaxes. Even then I'm the one taking it slow as I pull off his cock, tongue lapping at any remnants left behind.

"That was fun. We should do it again." There's a smugness in my tone. Ledger losing control before me, how could there not?

"We will, but first, I'm gonna eat your pussy till you come all over my face, juices dripping all over me, and coming like you never have before," he promises.

"God, yes," I moan, feeling the rasp of his tongue on my clit again.

"Fuck the alphabet, butterfly. I'm going to use numbers, memorizing each sequence that gets you off only to do it again." My eyes close, and I let him take control of my body. Ledger is hypnotizing me with his fingers and mouth, noticing when my eyes flutter open on one precarious sweep of his tongue, fingers sliding in and out of both holes. That his cock is hardening again doesn't hurt either. My body rocks back to meet each and every motion, and when I come, it's on a long moan as I call out his name, one hand gripping the sheets, the other on his leg, digging into his flesh hard enough I'm sure there'll be marks later.

20

TULSA ROSE

I pull into the home Ledger grew up in before he bought his place next to ours the next morning. I've got another mission ahead of me. A quick phone call to my therapist talking to her about the past few days helped tremendously. After that call, I was on the phone with Nelle to tell her about my night with Ledger, a replay of what I spoke to my therapist about. Only with Nelle, I told her how the night ended. The way she yelled, "Yes, Tulsa Rose!" into my ear, I'd say she was happy that things were finally falling into place. Except for where I am right now. When I kicked Ledger to the curb, I did the same to his mom, and I've got a lot to atone for.

"Are you just going to stay in there all day, or are you going to get your butt inside?" My door is open, one foot in, the other out, in case I needed to make a fast getaway when Ledger's mom, Heather, swings open her front door and calls me out.

"Coming!" I slide out of my Tahoe. Today's outfit is another tank top, this time matched with a skirt that stops midthigh, and flip-flops. When you're coming to Heather's with your tail between your legs, the least you can do is not wear a pair of cut-off jean shorts. I close the door and take a tentative step away from my vehicle, worried how she'll take me showing up unannounced.

"About damn time. I had to hear Mrs. Marble tell me you were back in town. Not even my own son deemed it necessary to give me a call." That's how I'm greeted when I take my first step up the stairs, holding on to the railing with one hand. I deserve her irritation. I've made a lot of mistakes, errors in judgment, stayed away all because of my own insecurities.

"Your son has been hogging every bit of attention when I'm not working around the house." Heather, being her normal self, doesn't say a word. She's waiting on me. If anyone can read between the lines, it's her.

"I take it you two stubborn asses are finally working through the years of bullshit." Where Ledger is tall, muscular, and dark-haired, his mom is not. Heather is petite, much like me, blonde and green-eyed. Clearly, Ledger takes after his dad, minus the eyes. Heather handed him down her green eyes, sometimes more vibrant, depending on the sun and what color he's wearing.

"Do you want the diluted version?" I take another step up, hitting the landing when she finally takes a step closer, allowing me to take a deep breath for the first time since I pulled up to her house.

"I don't care what version you give me as long you do it while hugging me. Get over here, Tulsa Rose." She opens her arms, and I fly into them. Everyone I've seen since coming home has been more than welcoming. Granted, it's only been Ledger, Hank, and now Heather. "I'm an asshole, the biggest one of all. How you're even hugging me or talking to me right now, I have no idea. I'm sorry, Heather." This time, tears do not fall down my cheeks unchecked, probably due to the fact that I've done so much of it recently that I'm all dried up.

"Oh, hush, you're not an asshole." I snort. That's a massive lie. "Okay, fine, maybe a small one, but, honey, you've been through more in seventeen years than most have been through in a lifetime." She pulls back from our hug and holds my shoulders. Heather is one to talk. She's a military wife, lost her husband when she was young, leaving her a widow as well as a single mom.

"I'm still sorry. I should have called you. If anyone could have straightened me out, it would have been you. Though it did force me to find an amazing therapist, and my best friend, Nelle, was there for me, too."

"Good. The same can't be said for Ledger. So much like his father, eating, breathing, and sleeping that damn roofing company of his," she grumbles.

"Tell me about it. And Ella is working for him. Double ick. Does no one else need a job in this town?" I raise my eyebrows at her, knowing Ledger is going to be in a lurch come the end of the day. "Maybe you should work for him. The phone call I overheard made it seem like no amount of fun."

"You want me to work for my son? Are you trying to make me see my hair stylist every four weeks instead of the usual six? No thanks." I laugh. She'd do it, and we all know it. "And what did Ella do now that he might need a new secretary?"

"It's a long story. I hope you have a few hours." The rest of my day is clear, minus making a trip to the grocery store.

With Ledger being at my place, the food he stocked us up on is dwindling. Two turkey BLTs and half a bag of chips for dinner was basically a snack for him.

"Honey, I'm retired. All I have is time." She opens the door for us. Walking inside is like going through a time machine. Everything is the same, which is pretty damn perfect since fashion and design make their way back in a perfect circle.

"Good, you're going to want to hear this. Though, you know who probably knew everything all along?" I ask her back, walking behind her until we make it to the kitchen. The round table still sitting in the middle, light shining brightly through the bay window, the walls a creamy yellow.

"Mrs. Marble. She knows everything, including the fact that Ledger picked you up at Hank's, where your Tahoe stayed until closing time. The woman has eyes all over town." We laugh. She gets around easily, knows the small town of Orange Blossom's comings and goings, even when the trash men are later than usual to pick it up. One day, we'll all be just like her—older, retired, still hot rodding around in her cherry-apple-red car with the sunroof open, all while watching and listening for the latest news.

"If I have time today, I think I'll stop by her place, too."

"She'd enjoy that. Sun tea?" she asks. I nod, wiping my sweaty palms down the front of my skirt. I'm not sure if it's the right or the wrong thing to do, telling Heather about Ella and everything she's put Ledger and me through, but I've already opened that can of worms.

"Thank you." She bustles around the kitchen, grabbing the pitcher of tea, glass with yellow lemons all over it. Ledger's mom always steeped it in the windowsill above the sink. Tea bags, hot water, a heaping amount of sugar and sun was all it took to brew, pour it over ice in the mason jars she's collected throughout the years.

"You're welcome. Before we get into the drama, tell me what finally brought you home." The past is erased. She's not pissed about me never coming home, never calling her, texting, or any of the likes. It's like a clean slate, no time has passed, and she loves me, much like Hank. God, I love the two of them.

"Well, I knew Alabama wasn't going to be home forever. On a whim, I applied for a job at Repair and Restore, R & R, in town. I was surprised. All I did was send in my resume, they called me back, set up a time to have a meeting with them via a Teleconference, and I was hired on the spot with a two-week notice to get home before my first day." It took me a week to get things settled with Nelle, not wanting to leave her in a lurch with the apartment and dealing with my job at the time. They were reluctant to let me go, and I had to work double time to close out my projects in order to feel comfortable with leaving in a week. That's why I hit the ground running when I came back. The donation truck came earlier this morning, loading everything I set aside in bags, and the furniture in the house that could be put to good use instead of collecting dust. I still have to go through the shed and head into town to see Mr. Flay. Now that I'm home, it's time to put my trust to good use. It sits in the bank doing nothing but gaining interest. Thankfully, Montgomery was smart, invested wisely and took care of the monthly bills after Momma passed away. One day, I came home from school to find our house had no power, which also meant no running water. Ledger hadn't moved in at that time, so it's not like I could run next door to ask him, and the neighbor who lived there before wasn't the nicest. I called Montgomery. He came flying home, called the power company, paid the bill, and took over everything since then. He was wise beyond his years, putting a few things in place. The house was paid off well before he passed away. And just because we had money from our parents' passing away did not mean he spent it like it was water. Mont had mine put in a trust until I turned twenty-five. He bought me a used car, nothing fancy or expensive, buying more for safety than anything else. It sucked to lose my family, but I was fortunate that he had it set up to where I wouldn't fall flat on my face our lose our family home should I want to keep it, which I do, even if I refuse to move into the master bedroom. Since the only time I touched any money was during college days, there's now a pretty penny, and I'd like to help others who aren't as fortunate as me.

"I'm proud of you. Now tell me what Ella did this time." We spend the remainder of the late morning and early afternoon talking. Heather even does this humming when I tell her the reason why it was the last straw for Ledger when it came to Ella. My guess is that Heather will go work for Sinclair Roofing, regardless of the gray hair she'll receive.

21

LEDGER

"You're really firing her?" Chase asks me after we parked next to one another in the makeshift parking lot in the back of the lay-down yard. I'm sure Ella saw us pull through the gates after we went down to the jobsite we're starting on Monday. I've not been this nervous in a long damn time, but this one is fucking with me, has me worried and on the edge of my damn seat.

"Yep, it's one thing to fuck with me, it's another to fuck with Tulsa Rose." The only thing that calmed me down is the woman who's mine, she's been put through the damn wringer and still comes out swinging. A flick of her tongue across my lip, and that's all I could stand. She refused to let it only be about her, so we made it work that we both got ours. As hot as it was, each of us trying to get the other off first, it sucked my attention wasn't fully on hers the entire time, and vice versa.

"Alright, then, think we should bring another woman in on the mix in case she comes back with something foul?" Chase makes a great point, one I didn't think about, and I should have. There are only cameras on the outside of the building, pointing toward the yard and building where we stash our supplies for upcoming projects, not inside the office.

"Fuck, only person I can call is Tulsa, and she's with my mom today." I pull my phone out, ready to dial. "Let's go to the warehouse. I'll make a call, and we can stay away from the crazed lunatic."

"Good idea." Chase walks ahead. I unlock my phone with Tulsa's birthday set as the code. I never set up the facial recognition part after my last phone broke.

"Hey, your mom and I were just talking about you," Tulsa answers the phone. I've yet to talk to my mom, but knowing she gets all her damn information from Mrs. Marble, what was the use? Plus, I've been busier than normal, and not all of it was work.

"Shit, if you and Mom are done raking me over the coals, will the two of you meet me at the shop? Chase brought up a valuable point. Two guys telling her she's canned isn't a great idea." The scraping of her chair in the background tells me all I need.

"Yep, we'll be right there. Also, I told your mom about what's going on and how Sinclair Roofing might need a new secretary. You're welcome. See you soon," she says, then I hear, "Heather, we need to go rescue Ledger, and you're going to need to give the directions." After that, there's a click. She's hung up without saying goodbye. I put my phone away, shaking my head while grabbing the door handle.

"That's handled. I suppose we can go through the rest of the projects we've got going on, see where the crews are at and if we need to move things around. I'm going to be at the restoration project, be as hands on as I can," I tell Chase as I walk in.

"Already ahead of you. Grabbed the plans and orders." He points to the papers he has on the work bench. There's always something to be done. On the rare occurrences we finish a project early and one of the guys wants to keep earning money being paid hourly, this is where they'll be, organizing the warehouse, picking up shit that was left behind when we're all in a rush. It takes another thing off my plate and puts money in their back pocket, a fucking win in my books.

"Did you finish out that other estimate the other day?" I ask Chase. While I'd prefer to keep Sinclair Roofing to business only, we do pick up a few residential clients as well.

"Yep, they're waiting on a few other estimates and said they'd call us back. Your mom and Tulsa on their way?"

"They are. Pretty sure a speeding ticket would be the only thing that slows them down. Since Tulsa is driving and making her debut back in Orange Blossom, they'd probably give them a damn escort." Tulsa Rose has a way about her. Hell, so did her brother. It was the Williams. Everyone saw their struggles; all eyes were on them in a small town. They didn't let all the losses they were handed hold them back or allow people to show them pity. They grieved like anyone else would. Some people would go on benders with drugs and alcohol, but not Tulsa or her brother. Mont threw himself into raising Tulsa, and she did her best not to fall into a bad crowd, kept her head up and her eyes on the prize. I got it. When we first moved her to Orange Blossom, Mom was on her own, and I was the kid without a dad. It wasn't until Montgomery befriended me that I really started seeing what life would be like living in a community where everyone knows one another.

"That'd be some shit. Imagine Ella's face if she saw cops rolling in. She'd shit a damn brick." He's not wrong. When I had this place outfitted, I should have put cameras everywhere. Then we'd have our own view. "Hey, by the way, you take out the trash in the office, I've been thinking about your offer." Fucking finally. Now that Tulsa's home, I'd love someone reliable who can help out around here.

"You ready to take the position?" We were looking over plans, my eyes glued to another project that's going to be a nightmare; I can feel it. Another abandoned home that was foreclosed, sitting for years, a total re-roof with a bunch of damn valleys and dormers. The new owners wanted it shingled, then called and asked for a quote for metal.

"I am."

"Fucking finally. You can take on this job, too. That customer is going to be a pain in my dick." I stick my hand out. Chase shakes it, and I pull him in for a one-armed hug, damn happy that he's finally stepping into a position he was made for.

"Yeah, sure, whatever. You just don't want to deal with the residential shit. Maybe we can break that up, and if I'm slow on that side, I'll help you with the business projects," Chase offers.

"Fine with me. We'll figure out the logistics. Ready to clean house? I hear my woman's truck rolling up, and after the shit we shared last night, I'm pretty sure Tulsa would snatch Ella bald headed for the shit she's pulled." Tulsa could probably sweet talk her way out of a lot, but I'm thinking even the local sheriff wouldn't be able to sway Ella from pressing charges.

"Tulsa Rose is feisty. She'll come at you when you least expect it. I watched her do it to a girl in high school who was talking shit and making fun of another kid. If you didn't see it with your own two eyes, you wouldn't believe it. She slid her foot out, and the girl went down in front of everyone. Gave her a dose of her own medicine. Then Tulsa turned around like nothing ever happened."

"That sounds like her." It also goes to show you why she had a problem with Ella when Montgomery had her coming around all those years ago. My butterfly, she doesn't take any shit, another reason why she stayed away as long as she did.

22

TULSA ROSE

"**B**utterfly." My Tahoe is barely in *Park* when my driver's side door is open, and Ledger is moving inside the truck. My eyes lock on his, watching as his head dips, lips going to mine, giving me no time to prepare for the kiss he lays on me, and doing it right in front of his mother. My eyes close, and I sink into the moment. I missed the feeling of this even though I had it this morning before he left to stop at his house to get ready and then head to work.

"Ledger."

"I needed your lips. This is not going to be pretty. I'm going to need both of you to keep your cool. Bail isn't cheap, and she's going to do her best to fuck with your head. Don't let her control you." He has me in a stupor from the kiss he laid on me.

"I've got enough money to bail me out. I think we'll be fine," I tell him, looking over my shoulder at Heather. She smiles, an expression that more than likely mirrors my own.

One that says 'let Ella come at me.' We'll take the trash out in a way Ledger couldn't even if he wanted to.

"Fucking Christ, you two are not getting involved. You're here to make sure Ella doesn't try to start shit and make something out of nothing," Ledger states.

"Fun sucker. What did I tell you, Tulsa?" Heather says. I snicker. She's in her fifties and is acting like she's my age. I love her. "Fine, we'll be on our best behavior, I suppose."

"Thank you. What about you, Tulsa?"

"Who, me?" I hold my hand to my chest, mock horror that I'd start anything.

"Damn women," he grumbles, running his hand through his hair, acting like he's annoyed when there's a smirk on his face. I take the keys out of my ignition and move my body so I can slide out of the driver's seat. "Behave." Ledger winking for good measure doesn't help matters. Neither does his hands going to my hips, practically picking me up, causing me to wrap my arms around his neck, keys dangling from the tips of my fingers.

"What if I don't want to behave?" I watch as he lowers his head. His lips graze my ear, his beard rasping against my skin, causing a tingle to work its way through my body. I close my eyes, tip my head back to give him more room. The squeezing of his fingers along my hips only adds to the effect of making me want him more, even if it isn't the time or the place for my nipples to pebble, pussy to dampen with desire. He's not unaffected either judging by the deep breath of air he inhales.

"Butterfly, you're tempting the beast. Don't think just because my mom is here, I won't take you to my office, hike this cute-as-hell skirt up, and fuck you against the door." Great now I'm going to have to walk in, and face the she-devil with wet panties, "First, we need to take out the trash, and in order for me to do that, you'll have to play nice so I can take you home and we can play dirty." He nips the skin beneath my ear. The visual he described plays like a reel in my mind, doing nothing to stop the desire strumming through me. "Come on, butterfly, I'll make it worth it."

"Fine, but I swear to God, if she makes one comment about Montgomery, I'm going to pop off." There's only so much I can take. Speaking about my brother, who can't fight fire with fire, it's one of those subjects I can't contain my anger over.

"Alright, little hellcat, retract your claws. Let's get this shit over and done with, then the weekend is ours." He lowers me to the ground, hand going to my back, and walks me toward the door. Chase rounds the corner. A thought comes to mind. He and Nelle would be beautiful together. If we weren't dealing with Ella today, I'd be rubbing my hands together, walking back to my truck, grabbing my phone, and sending her a text with an image of the tall, blond-haired, blue-eyed man.

"Long time no see, Tulsa Rose," Chase says in a greeting.

"It's been a while. Ledger didn't mention you two work together." It makes sense, though, with all the construction classes he took in high school.

"Yep. Have been for a while now. Momma Sinclair, looking pretty as usual." He moves toward Heather and gives her a one-armed hug.

"Chase, you're a smooth talker. I hear you two will be looking for a secretary. If this one here didn't take a new job already, she'd fit right in and keep the two of you on the straight and narrow." Okay, absolutely not. I love Ledger, but working with him? No thanks. Plus, I have no idea about the ins and outs of anything roofing related unless it's designed in a way that has rich history. All of the layers of a home, I've got zero idea.

"You did this, didn't you? Planted a seed in Mom's head?" I don't respond, a good thing, too, so it seems. Ledger opens the door to the office, and a slew of emotions come flying back to the surface. Ella sits behind the desk, having a front row seat in Ledger's life for seven years. I'm not saying him reading the letter back then would have helped, which by the way, he's yet to read and refuses to. We both forgave one another. Yes, it was short lived for me to keep him at bay. It's kind of hard to do when the man is a wrecking ball, doesn't take no for an answer, and won't give up.

"Oh, yay me. The whole family is here. Obviously, Tulsa didn't get the message the other day when she called, and I told her you were too busy. Montgomery may have been blind, but I wasn't. How you two looked at one another when you thought no one was watching was disgusting," Ella says, full of disdain, acting as if we had some illicit affair when I was underage. The woman is delusional. Why be around Ledger for as long as she has if that's how she really feels? Unless you can't get the one you want because he's gone, so you go after the next best option—the best friend.

"Ella, you're fired. I'll give you two weeks' pay. Pack your stuff. It's time for you to leave." Ledger doesn't leave any room for negotiation even if I have to bite my tongue the entire time. I'd love nothing more than to lash out at her. Sadly, I know it wouldn't get me anywhere.

"You'll regret this. Just you watch, Ledger Sinclair, you and your little slut deserve one another. Montgomery would never allow the two of you to be together." We both have letters that state otherwise, but she doesn't know that, and I refuse to give her any piece of my brother.

"That's enough, Ella," Heather states, vehemence in her tone. Momma bear in full protect mode, she walks in making her presence known. Heather and Ledger might not have been born and raised here in Orange Blossom, but that doesn't make a difference when you've been a pillar in the community, helping your locals out, donating your time, giving them jobs, and going so far as to re-roof a family's home at cost or nearly nothing when they didn't have the money at the time to pay for it.

"I do have one question, Ella. Were you really ever pregnant with Montgomery's child?" If she was, a part of me would honestly ache for her. Losing someone so precious to you, born or unborn, is hard. I witnessed it firsthand with my best friend, watched her mourn like you would a person you've known your whole life. Grief is a bitch like that.

"Tulsa," Ledger warns under his breath. Either way, it's going to hurt. May as well rip the Band-Aid off in one go.

"You'd love to know, wouldn't you?" Ella stands up from her chair behind the desk. The computer is off to the side, paperwork on top, nice and neat, making it appear like she's organized when everyone in this room is knowledgeable in the fact Ella barely does her work. I watch her, the mannerisms, the low-slung shirt that gives more than a hint of cleavage, the short skirt, and sky-high heels. Everything clicks into place, the reason why she returned my letter, how she tried to tear me down when I was sixteen, and how I knew she wouldn't tell Ledger I called him.

"Actually, I don't need to know. Not anymore. You never loved Montgomery; he was a means to an end for you. I bet you were after Ledger all along."

"Oh, shit," Chase says, arms crossing over his chest.

"I'm also willing to bet you weren't ever pregnant, and that's low, really low, even for you." With that, I'm through. I'd like to say I knew my brother like the back of my hand. In a sense I did, so for him to stay with Ella after he figured out how cruel she really was, it's highly doubtful they continued further on.

"You're nothing but a little whore, thinking you have everyone in this town wrapped around your finger, having Ledger always going after you, every single month. Everyone knows you were his little side piece while you were gone. It's all too telling." My eyes go from his to Ledger's, unaware of what she's talking about. I stagger backwards. The man I've loved for, well, ever catches me and pulls me closer to him, wraps his arms around my chest and steadies me all while I have more questions and no answers.

"That's enough, Ella. If you won't leave now, I'll call the Sheriff and have you escorted off the property, then charge you with trespassing." I close my eyes, abhorring myself for hating Ledger even though the entire time I was gone, he was near me in a way I never knew. Ella grabs her purse and walks around the desk. All four of us take a step back so we're not in her path. No reason to get any closer than necessary to the vindictive bitch.

"And for your information, I had an abortion," are Ella's parting words, sucker-punching me in the gut. As much as I want to believe Montgomery wouldn't have dipped his wick without a condom inside Ella, it could be the truth, and now I have the ick once again.

"Well, this has been fun. I should have grabbed a bottle of Jack Daniels on the way out of the house," Heather says, remaining more composed than me.

"I think there's one in Ledger's office from the last issue the company had," Chase says.

"Good, we're going to need a few shots," Ledger says. I turn around, my head lifting to his, his arms still wrapped around my body. Mine do the same, and everything fades away. He tips his head, letting me know everything is okay, and with Ledger in my heart, I know it will be.

23

LEDGER

"**I** 'm tired yet wide awake." We're lying in my bed. There's only so much I can take on her too-small mattress at her place. We're both naked after taking a shower together. I thought she'd be plum worn out after I kept her body against the tile wall, legs hitched around my waist, the underside of my cock sliding along the seam of her pussy, and I watched her head tip back as she came, my cum coating her pretty body.

"You keep rubbing your slit against me, and I'll tire you out since the shower didn't do enough," I tell her, rolling us until I'm between her thighs, sitting on my knees, and holding her open for my viewing pleasure.

"Too bad you're all talk. You've yet to slide inside of me, Ledger. Why is that?" She's right. I haven't yet. There's a reason behind that matter, one I'm about to deliver, no matter how blunt it is.

"You want the truth? I'll tell you the truth, Tulsa Rose. The second I get my cock inside your sweet cunt, I'm not leaving. You're not on birth control, there will be no damn condom between us, and I'm not pulling out either, which means I'll fuck my cum into you until you're full of me, tying you to me in the basest way possible. Not giving you an option either. If you want my cock, it comes with possibly planting a baby inside your stomach." I should have known the beauty lying beneath me, hair spread out along my pillow, hazel eyes riddled with nothing but lust, lips plush and blowing out a puff of air not in disgust but in desire. Fuck me, Tulsa Rose was made for me, made for my cock, made for my heart, and made for my soul.

"Ledger, I wouldn't be in bed with you right now if I wasn't willing to give you the biggest piece of myself. My heart is yours, my body is yours, and damn it, my love is yours. Now, please put your dick to good use and get inside me," she all but demands, lifting her hips and situating herself at the tip of my cock. I sink inside, and there's no damn way I'm taking this slow. It's going to be hard and fast, working her body so hard that come tomorrow, she won't be able to walk without feeling a tinge of pain.

"Fuck, yes." One hand goes to her lower abdomen, holding her where she is. My other hand goes to her leg, throwing it over my shoulder. "Plant your foot on the mattress, Tulsa, and don't move it," I demand. Her body is virginal tight, and I've only got the tip inside of her. I'm not bringing up her past. There's no damn need, and it's not like I don't know. I know everything about my butterfly.

"Ledger, quit talking and start moving." Her attitude comes out to join the party. My eyes float from her face down to her bare cunt, lips inflamed and sucking at my cock, like the greedy things she is. I surge. One deep thrust, and I'm buried inside the woman I'd sell my soul to the devil for. The rippling around my length has me holding back from pulling out to carry on the motion over and over again. Her mouth is shaped like an *O*, and I realize this is what she wanted, only her body isn't used to the roughness. It doesn't matter that my tongue has been inside her, same goes for my fingers, stretching her pretty cunt every chance I get. The toys she brought over were a fuck of a lot smaller, too. She is going to feel the effects of me taking her for days.

"You good, butterfly?" I ask, my mouth grazing a kiss along the inside of her calf as I allow her to get used to my size, killing me while doing so. It's a necessary evil. Tulsa may not be a virgin, but damn if it doesn't feel like she is.

"So good." I adjust, pulling back slightly before pushing back inside, swiveling my hips, giving her the slightest friction against her pretty clit that has my mouth salivating for another taste of her sweetness. That will have to come later. Right now, we're both chasing a high.

"Fuck yeah. The way you feel around my cock, coating me. Look at you with your fists gripping the sheets, body tipped back, thrusting those pretty tits of yours, butterfly." I squeeze her thigh, adding to the multitude of marks from before. She loves to look at them in the mirror while getting ready for work. I know by the clenching of her thighs when I come up behind her, watching as she traces each and every one.

"Oh God, it's so hot, you're so hot, Ledger." Her hands leave the sheets and grasp the backs of my thighs, pulling me closer, as if that's even possible. The only time I'm away from her is when I'm pistoning my hips, dragging my cock along the walls of her pussy. Her velvet heat is gripping me so tightly, I know it won't be long till she comes all over me. I press on her lower stomach, wanting to see her gush, knowing she's capable of squirting. I want another first with her. Christ, the way her ass took my thumb, sucking me in until she was writhing on my face, my girl likes it dirty, and it's a good damn thing, too.

"Tulsa," I grunt. Her tits bounce with one powerful movement of my body. Her eyes shutter, eyelashes fanning along her cheekbones. A pretty blush appears along her cheeks and travels down the slope of her neck until it reaches the top of her breasts. Son of a bitch, it's taking all my control not to come with the way she looks right now. A living, breathing fantasy coming to life, blossoming before my eyes. "You ready, butterfly, ready to come on my cock, take my seed along with my baby?" She doesn't have to respond. She bears down on my cock, hands leaving my legs and going to her sweet tits. I watch as she pinches and pulls on the cherry-tipped nipples. That's all I need. I rock back and forth, keeping up the momentum, making sure her clit gets the friction she needs, hand holding her steady. One powerful thrust later, and she's coming all over my cock, her pussy, and our thighs. My girl, fuck, she astonishes me with how she takes me.

"Ledger!" The scream is ripped from her lungs. My head is thrown back as her tightness takes me for a ride, one I don't ever want to get off. Each thick rope of cum paints her depths. My hand stays steady on her stomach, this time not holding it down to make her orgasm that much better; it's in hopes that we created a baby. Wouldn't that be something? Our first time together, and she becomes pregnant.

"Tulsa." Even after I finish coming, I keep moving my hips back and forth while looking at our combined bodies. "I want a picture of us." I fall to my elbows, caging her in. "Would you let me, butterfly, hmm? Let me keep a precious moment between the two of us?" I ask her. She must like the idea. The pulsing of her center around my length gives it away. "No one will see it. It's for our eyes only." She locks her legs around my waist, her hands leaving her tits, one going to my bicep, grasping it, the other hitting the nightstand, wrapping her pretty fingers around my phone before handing it to me.

"It's yours, Ledger. Don't you know that by now? Every bit of me is yours, just like you're mine." I kiss her, tongue sliding out to lap at her lower lips, silently asking her to open for me. She does without hesitation. It's soft and sweet yet still powerful as hell. When I pull back, she groans at me pulling away, as if I could fucking ever. I'd follow her to the ends of this earth. She's never leaving my side again.

"Fuck yeah, I am. Keep your legs locked around me. Those pretty thighs are spread wide open." I take the phone, pull up the camera app, and take a picture of the two of us, of our combined wetness, while slowly moving, capturing the full effect of my cum coating the lips of her pussy.

"Ledger," she moans, and I know this won't be the last time I capture me fucking my woman on camera, especially since she's enjoying it just as much as I am.

24

TULSA ROSE

This morning is the first day of my new job. Starting in the middle of the week is awkward. Waking up with Ledger's head buried between my thighs wasn't. Honestly, he gave me the best sendoff ever, and when I attempted to return the favor, his phone rang, and he was flying out of the bed, realizing the time and how long he spent with me in bed after his alarm went off. The bad part about that was waking up when he did. It was early. A construction job of any kind doesn't have a certain set of hours. There's no nine to five, ever. It's from sunup to beat the heat till sundown, and that's only because it's too dark, along with the mosquitos that would carry you away come the witching hour here in Florida.

I drove into town and headed to the home office of R & R to get my paperwork, tax information, and where my desk would be should I want or need to work in the office. This job gives me the flexibility to work from wherever, though for the most part, I'll be at the Mockingbird House, searching online and in stores to find items that replicate the era of the home. A quick rundown of how a few things are handled, then I was in my Tahoe, ready to get my hands into the mix of things. Pictures and videos of the house were sent my way, but they never do a historical home justice. The walls tell a story, and the woodwork is a craft of its own. Nothing was used except their hands, tools, and a lot of time. Unlike today, where everything is machine driven.

What I don't expect when pulling onto the project, is seeing Ledgers big white truck or him standing next to it, shirt pulled up as he wipes the sweat off his face, showing me the flex of his abs. He almost has me forgetting to put my vehicle in *Park*. I'm too busy salivating over the man who currently has me walking bow legged after last night, only making it worse as he spread my thighs, hands and fingers digging into the insides to keep them open the way he wanted me. The bruises he left between them make me want to drop to my knees and beg for more. I finally pull my shit together and put the truck in *Park* this time, then grab my bag that holds my iPad, notepads, portable charger, and a whole lot of swatches for the exterior paint job they want started as soon as the roof gets under way. That's my first task. Which, obviously, Sinclair Roofing is doing. Smart move. Clearly, talking about our jobs wasn't high on the list of priorities. Ledger whispering into my ear that his sole purpose was to feel me come on his cock while he fucks his cum into my body with the very likelihood of us creating a child was. Yep, trying to explain to myself why I loved the idea of that wasn't a hardship either. I somehow manage to get out of my vehicle without stumbling. Ledger takes that moment to strip his cotton shirt off his body, throwing it into the truck and walking toward the front. He opens the door, grabs another shirt, and slides it over his head, this time giving me a show of his muscular back. The man is built from hours of hard work on the job as well as in the garage at his place, converting it into a gym of sorts. Though, I've yet to see him use it. I really hope to, and soon.

"Are you following me, Tulsa Rose?" I stop halfway to his truck when he turns around, taking a long leisurely look at me. I'm not in anything spectacular—a black blazer, white body suit beneath, jeans, and a pair of loafers. I was going business casual while staying comfortable to walk the house. That being said, a decent shoe was necessary, meaning heels were out. Thank goodness they're pretty, but they're not comfortable. Flip-flops were a no-go with construction happening everywhere, so I compromised and went with a hard-sole shoe that is cute and functional.

"Just making up for all the times you followed me," I toss back. We've yet to discuss that little bombshell. Ledger smiles at me and meets me where I've stopped. His hand wraps around my waist, and he pulls me into his body and drops a kiss on my mouth, claiming me in front of both of our companies. Though, he's his own boss, and mine isn't here, luckily. Still, Ledger makes it quick.

"I didn't realize you were working on the Mockingbird House," he says, hair mussed from wearing a hard hat, which reminds me that I'll more than likely need one myself to do my walkthrough.

"The same could be said your way. Are you here for the day or on to the next job?" I ask him.

"I'm here for the entirety. I was changing for a meeting. I'm assuming it's someone from your office." My eyebrows bunch because I didn't get any memo that I'd have a meeting with anyone on my first day.

"Hmm, I have no idea. I'm about to do a walkthrough, figure out a few things and go from there. I'll be around if you need anything." I go to my toes. Ledger gives in to what I want, but this time it's me making it quick, just in case my boss arrives on the job. That would be awkward, especially on my first day.

"I'll go in with you. The guys are working on the tear-off. It's going to need more wood than we thought. Mom is going to bust my balls when I ask her to do a rush order." That is one thing we all talked about after having a shot of whisky, her taking on Ella's old job a few days a week. It's been smooth sailing ever since. Heather comes in a few hours in the morning, gets whatever necessary items done, then leaves.

"I'd like that. Do you have a spare hard hat, or did the general contractor leave any? I forgot to grab one from the office," I ask as we walk toward the early 1900s home. Seeing the bones of this place is going to be amazing, and hopefully, I can talk them into sanding the trim down instead of painting over it, like so many others have before our company came through. From the pictures, it has about eighteen layers of paint too many.

"I don't. The GC has a few sitting out. He just left for the day but should be back tomorrow," Ledger says. His hand is on my lower back. The fabric doesn't hinder the heat he permeates whenever he's nearby.

"Thank you. If I were you, I'd call your mom soon, or she'll be done for the day. We all heard her loud and clear. She doesn't mind helping out, but she won't live at that office."

"I'll walk you in, let you do your thing, and then make the call to Mom." I don't respond, so lost in the beauty of the architecture in front of us as I take it all in. It's going to transform into a labor of love, with a lot of work. My hands are itching to get started.

25

TULSA ROSE

After walking through the Mockingbird House, looking at everything that needed to be done, making notes on my iPad, recording notes in my phone, I headed back to my Tahoe. I'm using it as an office of sorts, so lost in my work it scared the shit out of me when Ledger came up to say goodbye. He was reluctant to leave me alone at the house. I kissed him, soothing that alpha inside of him. It wasn't like I was staying much longer anyways. I had to go back to the office, drop off a few revisions, and then meet Ledger at his house, which is where I'm headed now. Well, after stopping at my place, shucking the work clothes, pulling out another tank top, cut-off jean shorts, and flip-flops. I didn't even bother packing clothes for work tomorrow. I'll just stop by my place and change after Ledger is off to work.

Now, I'm pulling into Ledger's driveway. His garage door is open, and he's currently doing a pull-up, legs crossed at the ankle, shirtless, only wearing a pair of shorts. The sweat is glistening along his back. I watch the sinewy muscles as he lifts his body up with ease. The heavy metal is thrumming through the speakers as I open my door, slide one foot out and then the other, closing the door gently as not to interrupt him. The heat from the sun feels good on my skin as I walk closer. He's got dimples in his lower back. My gaze moves up toward his upper back. His shoulders are broad, carrying more than just his body around. They carry the load of life, taking everything on, acting like it doesn't weigh him down. His arms hold me without hesitation, a good day, a bad day, no matter the reason. If I'm near, he's got his arms wrapped around me. His hands are currently wrapped around the bar, helping him lift and lower himself, calloused from all the work yet touching me in only the way he can. The truth of the matter is that his hands, his fingers, his lips, his whole body anywhere near mine sends a hyper awareness through my body.

I make my way until I'm inside his garage-turned-gym. The beat of the rock music vibrates the concrete beneath my feet. Still, Ledger is pushing his body further than I could ever imagine. I'm about to take a seat on the weight bench when he lets go of the bar and lands light on his feet. He turns around, not surprised that I'm standing in the garage.

"Enjoying the show, butterfly?" It's hard to hear him over the music. Good thing I can read lips. Speaking of, mine are suddenly dry at seeing his hair slick with sweat, messy in the way the strands aren't lying in their normal way. The look on his face shows a craving that I know is consuming me. His five-o'clock shadow surrounds his mouth, and Jesus, his chest. My thighs tighten. My knees lock. I'm pretty sure that was me who let out a mewl of sorts. "Fuck, yes, you were." Light on his feet, he prowls toward me, confident in knowing what he does to me.

"Ledger." His hands wrap around my hips, then slide beneath my tank top, pulling it up and over my head. I didn't bother with a bra when I got re-dressed. His nostrils flare, tongue licking his lips, and his head dips down. I think he's going to kiss me, am prepared for him to make me breathless. Instead, he lowers his head further and wraps his mouth around one nipple, sucking the tip deep into his mouth. My hands delve into his hair, holding him to me, unwilling to let him go. My thighs quiver from pressing them together in order to somehow quench this need for him whenever I'm around him.

"Butterfly," he whispers along my heated skin. A different type of sheen appears before me, one not from working out but from a need that only Ledger can create inside of me.

"Don't stop," I whimper. His mouth moves away from my breast. Cooler air hits the sensitive bud. He moves to the other while his deft hands work the button of my shorts. I watch the entire time as his eyes stay on mine, his cheeks hollowing out with each deep pull around my nipple. The sensation carries down to my core. Ledger pushes the jean material down my hips, leaving me in only my thong as I step out of my flip-flops. The black gym mats beneath my now bare feet are warm from the weather, adding to the euphoria of this moment. The calloused hands I was admiring wrapped around the metal bar are now cupping the cheeks of my ass, pulling them apart, his fingertips sliding around until they graze the wetness as I widen my stance.

"I can feel how wet you are for me, and I'm going to watch as that pretty pussy of yours takes my cock," he states, then he rips my panties down my legs until they're in a torn puddle. His thick cock points up, the waistband of his shorts unable to hold it back anymore, and I watch as he takes care of his shoes and socks, shucking off his shorts. Now we're both completely bare. "You like that, don't you. I can see your wetness coating your inner thighs, making me want a taste. I do that, it'll be too damn long until I feel your heat surrounding my cock." He takes my hand and leads me to the weight bench I was going to sit on to enjoy a show. He lies down on it, legs on either side, his length flat against his lower abdomen, and pulls me toward him. I lift one leg. Ledger's hands settle on my hips once again, his eyes locked on my dripping wet center as he guides me to where he wants me, sliding along the underside of his cock. His groan matches my moan as I rock my hips, edging closer to the thickest part of him. Being teased is fun and all, the buildup, the foreplay, it's a heady sensation, but what I really want is him completely inside of me.

"Look at you, dripping wet. You want my cock, butterfly, get on it."

"You don't have to tell me twice." Lifting away from him makes me want to cry, almost. I use my thigh muscles, still feeling the burn along with walking bowlegged after what seems to be our marathon of sex in the past twenty-four hours. We're making up for lost time. Ledger seems to have something to prove about the one and only time I was with someone else. And don't get me started on the fact that I'm sure Ledger wasn't a monk. There are some answers a woman does not want, one of those being past partners. Triple ick. My hand wraps around his thick length. The tips of my fingers barely reach around to touch. He's that big.

"Christ, Tulsa Rose, the view I have right here." Once the head of his cock is inside me, my hands move to the tops of his thighs. The grip he has on my hips tightens further as I keep my feet planted, using my lower body so slide down another inch, still unaccustomed to how big he feels inside me.

"Ledger." My eyes close, head tipping back, as I slide down further. The way my walls ripple around him, I can't stand it anymore. I let my body drop, taking the full length of him inside of me.

"Soon, I'm going to see you swell with our child. With any luck, you're already on your way there. I'll be watching as your body transforms before my eyes, loving every fucking minute of it." His declaration, it does me in. I open my eyes. Ledger looking at me the way he is, I know more than anything just how deeply he cares for me.

"I love you," I say on a whisper, unable to hold the words in any longer, rocking my hips.

"More than words, that's how much I love you, Tulsa Rose. No amount of words will ever be enough to describe what I feel for you." He lifts his body up, still seated inside me, taking over as his lips land on mine. My tongue flicks out and glides along his as he leisurely devours me whole, consuming my body as well as my heart. What started off as a frenzied pace is becoming more of a delicious slow burn, and it's one we both need.

26

TULSA ROSE

"Tulsa Rose, I did it, can you believe it? I think I'm still in shock, and if you were here, I'd have you pinch me." I'm talking to Nelle a few hours later. My body finally said no more. Walking was painful, so much so that Ledger carried me out of the garage, through his house, up the stairs, and to where I'm currently soaking, phone on speaker and talking to my best friend. My pussy is literally battered and bruised. Ledger being Ledger is completely pleased with himself, walking around like a proud fucking peacock, naked, dick somehow still hard, and when he attempted to get in the clawfoot tub he added to his master bathroom, apparently, he renovated a few things in his house, the tub an added perk for me, I put my foot down, or tried to. Even that hurt.

"Oh my gosh, you're moving to Florida! You better move into my house. Don't even think about moving into town or getting an apartment. It's not like I'm there anyways, and it's mostly cleaned out." I sit up, water sloshing as I do, arms flailing, legs kicking. Thankfully, my phone is on the windowsill using the speakerphone, away from the tub and safe.

"What the fuck is wrong?" Ledger comes flying into the bathroom, this time in a pair of shorts instead of the naked form he tends to like whenever I'm around.

"Nelle is moving to Florida! Oh my gosh, I could cry. Life is coming together. Everyone I love will be here." Nelle lets out an audible breath through the phone. We both need each other, whether we wanted to admit it or not. Me leaving didn't help matters, even when Nelle pushed me to go home, to be where I belonged. It meant leaving her, and I've hated it the entire freaking time. Ledger is amazing in every way imaginable, but nothing takes the place of your best friend, bitching about life over drinks and greasy food, where you can watch a show that makes no sense to the outside world, but with the two of you, there are inside jokes galore.

"That's great, butterfly. Happy for you. Christ, I think I'm still recovering from the screaming. I thought you fell." He walks closer. I gingerly sit back, legs back in the water. "Hey, Nelle! Sorry to interrupt your girl time." He drops a kiss on my forehead and drags the tips of his fingers along the outside of my arm, awakening my body yet again. Too bad said body is completely out of commission. Even throbbing in need has me wincing.

"Hey, Ledger, no worries," Nelle replies. Ledger turns around and walks away. I drop my head back, close my eyes, and let out a low mewl once he's out of sight. I don't know who needs to be pinched more—Nelle or me.

"Oh, girl, you have it bad. I'm not even in the same room, and I can feel the chemistry between you two."

"So bad. The chemistry is apparently good enough to have me walking bow legged for days on end, too." Nelle chuckles, not a hint of feeling bad for me in her tone. Man, what does a woman need to do to get a bit of sympathy around here?

"That is not a bad thing to have. I'm happy for you, and I can't wait to meet the man who's kept your pussy locked up tighter than a nun's." A snort escapes me. It wasn't for lack of trying, especially the first year. I wanted to be young and reckless, have no remorse for any- and everything. Sure, I still remained the same at heart. My virginity I had control over. Fat lot of good that did. You learn a lot about yourself when you give an important part of yourself away. The only point you've proven is that you're an idiot and you'll never get it back. No one was hurt except me and my stupid pride.

"Needless to say, Ledger is making up for lost time, though I'm not sure on whose part—mine or his. Whatever the case, we're both reaping the rewards, except the place between my legs. Unimpressed is what she is, mostly because she's currently out of commission." Nelle and I have zero boundaries. We talk about any- and everything. Going to the bathroom, either one of us will walk in on the other, do our makeup, talk about the latest drama, it really doesn't matter.

"Now that we have that out of the way, are you sure staying at your house is okay?" For the first time, Nelle seems apprehensive. The excitement is gone from her voice.

"Oh my gosh, yes. Truth time?" I ask her so she knows I'm being serious.

"Always."

"I love my childhood home, the memories it holds, good and bad. What I didn't realize was as much as I love it, at the end of the day, it's a foundation, four walls, and a roof. Mont gave me first dibs on the master bedroom. I didn't want it then, and I don't want it now. It's a home that built me. As for staying in it forever, I'm unsure about the possibility. The home is bigger than a single person needs, plus it's not like I'm home. The last time I was there for more than twenty-four hours was the first two nights I was back in Orange Blossom. There's a certain man who has no problem consuming my time, and I rather like how he does it," I end on a sigh. Ledger and I have talked about our willingness to potentially conceive a baby, which I'm apparently all for, considering I'm the one begging for him to come inside me.

"So, what you're saying is?" Nelle asks.

"That I want you to move down to Florida, live in a house that should be lived in like a home, and please take which-ever room you want." I've still got a few things left to do around the house. This will light a fire under my ass and snap me into gear to get it done on the weekends.

"If you're positive." Nelle is treading carefully, worried I may break down.

"Nelle, get your cute booty down here. I'm hoping you'll love Florida more than Alabama and make this place your permanent home. Plus, I'm going to need your mathematical genius of a brain in a few weeks. I've got some big plans, and I know you'll be along for the ride with me." Seriously, the way things are progressing with Ledger and me, I'll be moved in here full-time. My family home will sit empty if Nelle doesn't take the bait to move in, and I'd hate for that to happen.

"Fine. This is going to require work. Are you sure you'll have time in between all the bed acrobatics?"

"Go away already. Asking dumb questions will get you dumb answers, Nelle. Tell me everything we need to do to get your down here. Oh, and before I forget, there's a single man who works with Ledger. He's my age, is becoming a partner at Sinclair Roofing, and from what I'm told, he's an absolute godsend with his niece. Ledger even has proof of the tea parties in the form of pictures. I'm introducing you to Chase the first day you're down here. I mean, think about it. We're best friends, and Ledger and Chase are best friends. This shit is going to happen; I don't care what you say. Plus, these Orange Blossom men do not disappoint in the looks department." Even Hank at his age is still a good-looking man. Another plan forms, one that may include Heather. Maybe I can get Ledger on board. Well, after we see them together first.

"Tell me what he looks like. Details, woman, details." Wow, she's more excited than I thought she'd be. Maybe her moving to Florida is for the best after all.

"Tall, blond, blue eyes, muscular, a mischievous grin. I'll try and sneak a picture to you the next time he's at the Mockingbird House." She makes a noise like Chase is her kryptonite. I knew he would be. The last guy Nelle was with was dark everything—hair, eyes, soul, you name it. The complete opposite of Chase or her usual she'd be attracted to. Also, a total loser. It was a fling that turned into something more when the condom broke, leaving a piece of her broken when she lost more than the weight of what would be a dead beat baby daddy. I'm not saying that lightly either. The man ran the second she told him about the positive pregnancy test, blocked her phone number, social media, and if we ran into him, he'd ignore her. I've got more than a four-letter word when it comes to potential parents like that.

"I see you have scouted thoroughly, and I appreciate your diligence." Nelle talks as if this is a business plan.

"Oh my gosh, go away with that talk. My water is getting

cool, and the last thing I want to be is cold. I'll call you tomorrow on my way to work. Text me the details on what you need set up at the house, and we'll make it happen." I'd usually add hot water, prolonging the process of leaving the comfort of the tub, but my grumbling stomach is giving me other ideas. It's saying, 'Feed me,' even though my center is thoroughly enjoying the long soak.

"I will. Love you, Tulsa."

"Love you. I can't wait till you're down here with me." We hang up after that. Coming home has helped more than just me; it's helping Ledger and Nelle, too.

27

LEDGER

Three Weeks Later

"Do you think it was a good idea to have the girls head to Hank's before we were done off-loading Nelle's boxes?" Chase asks me as we walk through the door. It's busier than it was than the last time I came in here to meet Tulsa Rose.

"Probably not. Knowing Tulsa and what I've heard about Nelle, the girls know how to have a good time. They deserve it, though. Tulsa has been on the edge of her seat ever since Nelle told her she was moving down." That was a few weeks ago. A lot of planning was involved, like a new Internet service for Nelle to have a secured line and replacing the pool system to salt since Tulsa knew they'd be using it more. One thing that didn't change was my woman sleeping in my bed every single night. Earlier this morning, she mentioned staying the night at her house so Nelle wouldn't get lonely.

That was fine with me, but I'd be right there with her. We compromised in the long run. We'll see how the night goes and how her best friend feels.

After the girls had the most of Nelle's stuff sorted, they agreed to figure out the logistics of duplicates later and stored what she didn't need right away in the spare room. Fuck, my butterfly worked like two grown men would, stating it was high time life was breathed back into the house. Nelle had her own furniture to bring in, and as far as Tulsa was concerned, she was tired of holding on to a house sitting empty with furniture that could be used. So, I made another phone call, and a few guys came out to help load up the truck with the living room, guest room, and her bedroom furniture and the rest of the stuff she wanted to get rid of. The master bedroom set she wanted to keep because it was her grandparents' before it became her parents', and then Montgomery's. There was no damn way I was letting her set it up in her bedroom when we'd be moving it again whenever she got it through her head where I want her, *always*. She'd be living at my house anyways, which is where it is now, in the once empty guest bedroom.

"Fucking Christ, who invited my mom?" I ask Chase as I open the door for him and see all three girls dancing on top of the bar. The crowd is getting a front row view, one of my woman in a tight fitting tank top, one I know she isn't wearing a bra beneath since she got dressed in front of me this morning, the cut-off jean shorts with pockets peeking out beneath the hem, distressed from wear and tear rather than the style you buy in the store, and on her feet are flip-flops you'll find her wearing whenever she's not at work.

"I'm willing to bet that would be Tulsa Rose. You're fucked, my man," Chase tells me as we walk further inside.

He's wrong. I'm not fucked. Tulsa is, or she will be the minute I get her away from prying eyes.

"She might have invited her, but I know damn well whose idea it was to get them dancing on a bar top." Tequila shots, Mom's preferred liquor of choice. And not the cheap variety. Nope, the smoother, the better, meaning she goes after the top-shelf tequila, and that shit will bite you in the ass if you're not careful.

"Let them have fun. You'll enjoy the view, and so will I." My eyes cut to Chase, making sure his gaze isn't anywhere on my girl. I'm a possessive fucker, and I'm not ashamed to admit it.

"As long as you keep them off Tulsa and my mother, you'll live to see another day."

"Dumbass, my eyes are on Nelle. I'm not looking at your woman." I walk toward the bar and hear him mumble, "I'm not a fucking idiot. Plus, she's like a sister." I smile, content with his answer.

"Ledger, Chase, what can I get you?" Hank yells out. The music coming from the juke box is turned up, a classic playing, singing about *the Earth was quaking, my mind was aching, and we were making it*. Tulsa's hands are above her head, hips swaying to the beat as she sings at the top of her lungs while looking at me.

"Beer. Bottle. They've been here, what? An hour, two tops. Do I want to know how many shots Mom bought the girls?" I ask Hank, taking my eyes off Tulsa for less than a minute to place my order and hear the answer. I'm sure they're three or four deep with zero fucking food in their stomachs.

"Your mom, that's the one you gotta worry about, bud. She's four shots deep. Tulsa and Nelle are only two. Neither of them want a hangover tomorrow. Their food is about ready. You want your usual?"

"Please, and thank fuck. Last time Tulsa tied one on, she had a hell of a headache and tried to run away." My hand wraps around her ankle once Hank moves to the cash register. The bar and grill is one of a kind here in Orange Blossom, serving food, liquor, and providing pool tables—a place for people to come and unwind. I settle on the barstool. My butterfly knows I'm here. Our eyes locked the moment I stepped inside. She was dancing before I got here, but I noticed the shift in her—the sway in her body intensified as she let her inhibitions drop now that she's got her man here.

She lowers her body. My hand moves off her ankle, and I sit back on the barstool. She's got my full fucking attention. "Hank, can you make our order to go?" I say to his back and see him nod. My eyes go back to the woman in front of me. Her body is flush from either dancing or me watching her dance, I'm not sure which, but I like it regardless, reminding me of how she looks when I'm buried inside her, breathless and blushing.

"You know, we're not the only ones who are about to leave. Do you see what I see?" Tulsa drops to all fours. A growl leaves my throat at the vision in front of me, her hair unbound and wild. My hand reaches out. She gets what I want and climbs down and into my lap.

"Tulsa Rose, all I see is you." Her arms loop around my neck, eyes full of mischief, and fuck me, I'm going to be in for it.

"Good answer, Mr. Sinclair. Though I was referring to the way Chase is looking at Nelle. I love a good matchmaking moment." She's been talking about this non-stop. I don't bother looking. Chase already admitted he liked what he saw when we walked into Hank's.

"Woman, leave them be. You've done everything you can, sending pictures of Chase to Nelle, getting on FaceTime so the two of them could meet. Now it's up to them." One of my hands wraps around her lower back, holding her in place, the other reaches for the beer Hank set down for me. "Now, I've got our food ordered to go. I'm going to enjoy my beer with my woman in my arms, then I'm taking you home. Hank has Mom, Chase has Nelle. Tonight is for me and you, no one else." The past few weeks, we have both been busy with work, then Tulsa had to get her house ready for Nelle, and then she was full of worry that Nelle wouldn't like it here. It's a huge change of pace to the city living she was accustomed to. Nelle is going to fit right in; all that worry was for nothing.

"Fine. There are still two more people who deserve to find a love like we have." She takes the beer out of my hand, brings it to her mouth, and tips it up. I watch her throat work the liquid down, and Goddamn if that doesn't remind me of how she takes my cock, sucking the cum right out of me. I take the bottle from her once she's done. Since it's now empty, I place it on the bar.

"Thanks, Hank." He sets our order down along with the bill. I pull out a couple of hundreds to cover what the girls started, our meals, and what I'm sure is to come.

"No problem, and you know that's too fucking much," Hank grouses.

"You taking Mom home?" He nods.

"That's not nearly enough, then. Thanks for watching out for her." I grab the bag and stand up, my hand moving down to Tulsa's ass. Her legs wrap around my waist, my other hand grabs the bag, and I carry both out of Hanks.

"Ledger, I can walk, you know," Tulsa laughs. "I know what you're doing. You're telling all of Orange Blossom who I belong to."

"Damn fucking straight," I reply with a straight face.

"I never thought I'd see the day that Ledger Sinclair would be staking his claim on me." Fuck, if my hands weren't full, I'd be doing a lot more than taking her lips with mine.

28

TULSA ROSE

"Are we ever going to talk about the fact that you were in Alabama once a month, every month, for ten years? That comes out to one hundred twenty days, give or take." We're slowly swaying on the front porch swing of Ledger's house. His home is practically a mirror image of my own, minus the pool and with a slightly different floor plan, plus he has a garage on the side of his house, and we have a covered carport instead.

"There's nothing to say. I did what I had to do," he states calmly. I lift my head from the crook of his shoulder. Ledger stays his stoic self, as if he wasn't practically creeping on me without my knowledge. Okay, he wasn't practically stalking. He totally was.

"And why do you feel like you had to check on me? If the roles were reversed, you absolutely would have been furious at me, chased me off back to Alabama with the sheriff escorting the way." He doesn't acknowledge me, too busy smirking at me, one hand on the ledge of the swing, the other playing with and softly massaging the base of my neck.

My legs are tucked beneath me, while his feet push us every so often to keep up the momentum.

"You'd be right about that, butterfly. Especially the first few years. There was a time when I wished you'd know I was there, but it never happened. I was lucky. I got to watch you be free, spreading those beautiful wings of yours." He looks down at me, lip twitching up in that almost smile of his.

"Huh, I suppose that's kind of sweet. You know, it would have been nice if you at least said hello or waved."

"Fuck no. I couldn't have. If I had, there's no way I would have let you go. All this would have been for nothing. You'd have either cried on my shoulder or kicked me in the nuts," he replies.

"Probably both. Did you ever read the letter I wrote you?" When I handed it to him, he tossed it out of the way, never said a word. I only noticed it was gone the next morning.

"Yep, sure did, then I put it in my safe. Keeping that forever. The first time you admitted you loved me, fucking has me right here, butterfly." He places my hand on his heart. The letter I wrote him said more than I'm sorry; it admitted my feelings from the very beginning, how I forgave him, then went on to say that it wasn't okay for me to blame him when he was only doing what Mont wanted, his last wishes.

"That's sweet, Ledger, really freaking sweet. And by the way, don't think your secret is safe. I know exactly what you did. Why I didn't so much as have a male study partner. It's a damn wonder I lost my virginity, and even then, it's questionable if you could even call it that." It wasn't until I found out that he was in Alabama once a month that the pieces started fitting together. I'd talk to a guy in class, things would go great, and we'd set up a study time or even a date if they could hold my attention long enough. The next thing you know, they were dipping out, suddenly texting they couldn't come or not showing up at all. After the fourth time, I quit trying. Why bother if that's how the little wanna-be men would act? Until I met Brody. He didn't scare away, but he sure enough didn't care about warming a woman up. A sloppy session with his fingers that had me turned off, the slide of a condom onto his cock before he surged in. Two thrusts later, and he was done. That's when I quit men all together, Nelle and I went to an adult store, had a lot of laughs, and a few toys later, I was ready to go. No man is worth your time if he's going to treat you like I was treated. I mean, Brody didn't even make sure I got off. After he came into the condom, he rolled away and fell asleep. I left as fast as he came, called Nelle, told her what happened, and went to the student health clinic for a test to be on the safe side. Nelle cussed up a storm, more annoyed about my first experience than anything. It was nothing a few drinks and my best friend couldn't cure.

"Little cocksucker. Saw you running out of his apartment, tucked into yourself, and knew something happened. A few minutes later, I knocked on his door, worrying he did something a fuck of a lot worse. Only took one look at him before he told me what happened, in a little too much detail. My fist met his face, then I left. Ate me up inside, and I had to leave before I did something stupid, like bang on your door and show you what it was like to be taken by a real man," Ledger admits.

"Huh, like punching a guy wasn't dumb?" I had no idea Ledger went to Brody's house; in fact, I never saw Brody after that one time. We didn't have classes together, so that was to be expected. We'd met at a smoothie shop on campus, and after I didn't see him there like I usually would, I assumed he was embarrassed. Evidently, it had a more to do with Ledger than anything else.

"It was worth it. *You're* worth it." He shrugs his shoulders like Brody couldn't have pressed charges on him. Men are so weird. Things that would eat at a woman seem to be a blip on their radar.

"Thank you, I think."

"No more talking about other men. You wanna talk to Nelle about it? Okay. To me, that part of your life is over. There's no need to discuss it anymore." I roll my eyes trying to conceal my laughter.

"So, since Chase took Nelle home, and Hank brought Heather home..." Ledger's eyes zero in on me.

"Jesus take the fucking wheel, my woman is trying to match-make every damn person in Orange Blossom," he breathes deeply, tips his head back, and tells the roof of the porch. Ledger may not have seen the way Hank looked at his mom, but I sure did. Nelle saw it, too. She was the one who nudged my shoulder when the two of them were talking as Heather tossed the shot of tequila back.

"Maybe Mrs. Marble will be next," I poke the bear. I can see the annoyance settling in. He is clearly done with my nonsense.

"Tulsa Rose, leave it alone. If Mom and Hank date, let them. At least let it happen on their own terms. As for Mrs. Marble, good luck. She's in a league of her own. Plus, do we know any man around her age who she'd be willing to date?"

"Who says he has to be her age? There are plenty of younger gentlemen here in Orange Blossom. Look at you, helping me. And they say romance is dead." He must be over my shenanigans, because his mouth closes in on mine, tongue flicking at my lower lip, demanding entrance. The hand that was massaging my neck is now holding me where he wants me, taking me like only Ledger can. My mind shut down everything else except the two of us, exactly what I need and want.

29

LEDGER

"Hey, Ledger, can we talk for a minute?" Tulsa rounds the corner coming off the stairs. I'm sitting on the couch, feet propped up on the coffee table, a hockey game on the television. The pro team from Tampa has been on a hot streak. Usually, I'd watch the game with Chase, but since it's Sunday afternoon and the last time I heard from him, he was with Nelle, I decided to stay home to watch it while Tulsa was working on her iPad.

"Sure. Everything okay?" I mute the television as she walks toward me, wearing one of my shirts and nothing else, her hair up in some kind of knot on top of her head with a pencil holding it in place. My hand reaches for hers. If we're going to talk, she's going to do it in my lap. Seems Tulsa had the same idea. She's sitting sideways, legs outstretched across the couch, her back on the tall arm rest, much like the back. There's nothing worse than having a low-slung couch, nowhere to put your head, and you're stuck holding it up instead of relaxing against it. She holds one of my hands. I move the other to her smooth upper thigh, wedging it between, feeling the heat I was able to lick, taste, and fuck earlier this morning. I bet if I checked right now, she'd still have the remnants of us from earlier.

"Yep. Got a bit of work done to stay ahead of the week and then was looking at the investment portfolio." Montgomery had it all laid out, allocating money each month into different funds, playing the market, and not conservatively. It's a wonder he wanted to clear land for a living. The man's mind was made for numbers. When he passed away, there were explicit instructions on how to handle the Williams' money. How much Tulsa could and should live off of during college, and the majority of it going to her when she turned twenty-five. It didn't go unnoticed that she didn't spend a fucking cent of it. If Montgomery were around, Tulsa probably still wouldn't have used the money. She made a name for herself when she worked part-time at the grocery store through high school, and she did the same thing in college, only as a teacher's assistant.

"Is there a discrepancy?" I receive the monthly emails, showing what profits were gained or if anything was lost. Other than that, Flay has a company handling the bulk of it. All I do is check to make sure there isn't a big chunk missing, and if there is, to backtrack it, usually to see the market took a dive. I'd like to think the investment company wouldn't fuck around, but you can never be too sure.

"Well, there's a lot of money in there. Money I won't ever be able to touch. The same could be said for any children or grandchildren we have. Plus, I'm not going to be that person who gives and gives to any child. All they would do is take. I was dealt a shit hand in a few aspects in life, but I didn't let it hold me back. Clearly, we had money. Montgomery never let on how much we had until the reading of the will, and he still made me pull my own weight. I paid half my car insurance, gas money, and if I wanted to spend money, I had to earn it. I'd like to instill the same in our own children. So, besides a pool, which we clearly need, unless you want me at Nelle's place ninety percent of the time, what are we going to do with it?" she questions. Tulsa is thinking about the future —children, grandchildren. Damn if that doesn't settle right in my soul.

"We'll get a contractor out here next week to add the pool. I want it enclosed with a safety fence around it that can be taken down once our children know how to swim. Anything else you want is up to you. We'll figure out how to deal with the financial side of shit later on." We live in Florida, so it goes without saying that any children we have will undoubtedly learn how to swim before they walk. "As for the money, it's up to you. Sinclair Roofing isn't a million-dollar business, but it does well for itself, enough to have the house and land free of a note, money can be set aside for a college fund, a trade, or God forbid they want to start a small business, without it hurting the bank."

"Okay on the pool, except I'm paying half, and I don't want to hear it. I've got to contribute somehow. Much like you, I've made good money along the way. This job makes it even easier. My Tahoe payment is a blip on the radar. Keeping it financed is what keeps my credit revolving. Other than that, I've got no major debt. Which leads me to the next subject, well, two actually. I want to rent the house to Nelle with an option to buy should she want it." I raise an eyebrow at her. Tulsa has been busy plotting and planning, and not only today but other days as well.

"I see nothing wrong with that. If Nelle doesn't want the house, you're keeping it, and we'll figure out what to do. The house is solid. Maybe one of the kids will want it later on in life."

"God, I love you, Ledger." Happiness shines through her voice.

"Love you, butterfly. What's next on your list? You said two things," I prod. My eyes glance at the score then move back to hers, giving her my full attention.

"Alright, I want to meet up with Flay. I'd like you to go with me. The pile of money, well, I'd like to see if we can help a local women's shelter. I drove by The Women's Center in town the other day during my lunch. It needs help and funding. The programs are outdated, and they don't have the supplies. I'd like to help them out. I've never done something like this before, and, well, your help would be appreciated." She shrugs her shoulders, a nervousness in her tone.

"I've got no problem going with you. Not sure they'll be excited about a man in their business, though." The Women's Center helps women get back on their feet while they recover from domestic violence, sexual assault. They counsel women who have gone through a hardship or trauma. "I'm not going to poke and prod. You're aware I have my resources when it comes to knowing everything about your time in Alabama. My guess is Nelle had something happen to her. I'm not asking for answers. All I'm saying is, I'd ask her opinion first."

"You're right. I'm going to. There's one more thing. This one, Nelle and I spoke about a little bit; The Women's Center we haven't yet, but I'll make it a point to talk to her. And for the record, it's nothing abuse wise; it's just not my story to tell." She puts her thumb and pointer finger together to emphasize it being a tiny subject. I doubt it's anything but small.

"Go on."

"It's going to take a lot more help and work that I have no idea what the hell I'm doing. There are so many kids around here. Some are fortunate enough to have family to help raise them, while others aren't. I'd like to set up a foundation for them. It's going to be a big undertaking logistics wise." There's excitement in her tone. Tulsa is passionate about the subject. It's a good idea. There's been a time or two we've worked on a big project, made a nice bonus at the end after paying out my employees then myself. A lot of the times, if there's not a big project looming at my house, I'd drive up to the local high school to donate to the kids' lunch accounts, making my way down the line to the middle school. The older kids get lost along the way. Don't get me wrong; a lot of the local folks help, but it's usually toward the elementary school age instead of teenagers.

"Set it up, make an appointment. Tell me the time, and I'll be there. Fuck, Tulsa, Montgomery would be right by your side doing this with you. He'd be so damn proud of you. Hell, I'm proud. Never change, butterfly." Her arms wrap around my neck, face buried in my neck, tears hitting my skin, and I hold the woman I love, unsure why she's crying. All I know is, when Tulsa needs me, I'm going to be there, every damn time.

30

LEDGER

I'm sitting at my desk, looking over the schedule for the week, checking what projects are where. Chase handling the residential side is shaping up to where we could potentially need to hire a whole other crew. I guess next on my agenda will be heading to the local high school, sitting down with a counselor to see if any seniors are looking to start a trade in roofing. We'll see how many want to start right out of the gate, then go from there to look in the community.

"Hey, Ledger, you got a minute?" I was so engrossed in reading through emails, schedules, and order sheets that I didn't hear Sheriff Judd open the door or walk through the office until he announced his presence.

"Hi, Judd, sure do. What's up?" He walks in further, hat in his hand, uniform on, and looking like he's got the type of news no one wants to hear. The last time Judd came around unexpectedly wasn't a great experience. Seeing him around town isn't a problem. Him coming to you? That's different. I pick my phone up, glance at it and see I've got a text from Tulsa. I relax

> Butterfly: I'm stopping at the grocery store. Is it okay to assume you'll grill dinner and I'll take care of dessert?

"Give me one second. Tulsa texted." Judd takes his seat in one of the chairs. The other one is currently covered in plans. The next time Mom comes in, I'm going to see if she wouldn't mind organizing a few things.

> Me: Sounds good. The only dessert I need is between your thighs. Call you in a few minutes. Judd is here.

"Not a problem. This won't take long. I know you've got your hands full. If you wouldn't mind telling Tulsa, I'm sorry I've yet to stop bye to say hello. The station has been a shit show—new recruits, false reports, and more paperwork than I ever care to deal with, but it comes with the job." Judd, Montgomery, and I all grew up together. It was him and his father who told Tulsa the news. Judd tried to get his father to wait until I made it to their place before telling her about Mont's accident. I went above him once the dust settled. He retired six months later. How that shit was handled was not right, not when he could have waited five more damn minutes. Judd took his place, thankfully not like his asshole of a father.

"I'm sure she'll understand. Tulsa hit the ground running herself the minute she hit Orange Blossom—us, her job, her best friend moving down here." I'm wondering why he's here in the first place. I see Judd at Hank's, have the occasional beer while watching the game or shooting the shit. And we see one another around town.

"I imagine so. It's good she's back home. It's where she belongs." I don't respond. On that, we can agree.

"Is there a reason you're here, Judd? I'm not trying to be rude, and I've got no problem catching up. Unfortunately, a Monday morning when the Mockingbird House has more shit wrong with it than we thought isn't the best time." Fucking water issues. The roof was well past its age, so we knew there'd be some issues. What no one expected was that it's rotted through a few of the trusses. Getting a crane scheduled and staying on schedule is damn near impossible now.

"Ella came in over the weekend. I wasn't on duty. My younger deputy took the statement. I'm here as a courtesy, to hear what you have to say, then I'll tell you what she's claiming."

"Son of a bitch. She was fired weeks ago. Ella was in a snit. Chase had a good head on his shoulders and had me call Tulsa. Mom was with her. All four of us were in the office when I let her go. A few words were said, and Elle called Tulsa a few names. Never before in my life did I want to hit a woman. That was the first time I really thought about doing it," I tell Judd. I'd have never done it, but Tulsa and my mom would have, if I didn't hold them back.

"I'm going to pretend I didn't hear that. You see, Ella came in with a black eye. She's claiming Tulsa Rose hit her at Hank's this weekend. She tried to snowball my deputy. He's a young one, has a lot to learn, was ready to go straight to Tulsa instead of taking the time to check out the facts. I stopped at Hank's early this morning. No idea why he was there at nine o'clock, but glad he was nevertheless." Jesus fucking Christ, this bitch has no damn sense.

"Hank was probably doing an order. The girls let loose Saturday night. Mom probably drank all of his top shelf tequila." Ella is a snake, first bullying Tulsa when she was younger, then being a certified cunt and returning the letter which was addressed to me, and again when Tulsa called after she returned and we were finally on the right damn path.

"That's what he said, well, not about your mom. The crowd got bigger, beer was consumed, a lot of food, so he was in there. Now, here's the good part. Hank told me Ella was at the bar after Tulsa and you left, said there was a fight. It wasn't with Tulsa, Nelle, or your mom. Ella and another woman got in a dispute. Hank broke it up, escorted both parties out of the bar." Ella likes to play. This time, it seems she lost at her own damn game.

"So, you see, I'm letting you know. I figured it'd be better for me to show up here, tell you, than to show up at Tulsa's place of employment or your house later tonight. The file is going to be taken care of. Ella will be slapped with a fine for filing a false report, using man hours when it wasn't necessary. The only problem I'm seeing is, this will create a domino effect. Either Ella will stop with this high school crap, or things are going to escalate. Watch your back. The fact that Ella is going after Tulsa when you fired her, it's messed up." I close my eyes. Tulsa Rose is going to lose her shit when I tell her the news, damn near a month later. We haven't heard or seen a peep out of Ella, then all of a sudden, over the weekend, this happens. This shit stinks to high heaven.

"Tulsa's going to be pissed. I never would have thought Ella would go after her. Me? Yes. Not the other way around. The whole reason for having an audience was in case of blowback. All I'd need is for her to try and pin me with a charge I'd have no proof I didn't commit. Now, it seems like I threw Tulsa out of the frying pan straight into the fire." I rub a hand down my face, wondering how to break the news to her, because there's no way I'll ever keep this from her, not when I've finally got her in my arms.

"Nah, she's a tough girl. She'll be alright. Anyways, I'm out of here. I'll take care of Ella, probably make an appearance at her family's sit-down dinner, scare her with the probability of jail time. I'm thinking the fine she'd only laugh about." Judd stands, and I do the same. Looks like I'll be delivering this shit to Tulsa at work, on a damn Monday no less.

"Thanks for telling me and not going to Tulsa first. I know you're breaking protocol, and, well, I appreciate all you've done, Judd." We shake hands. He's done a few things along the way, like the incident with the cleaners at Tulsa's house when she was in Alabama as well as a few others.

"The least I can do," Judd responds, then takes his leave. I grab my phone off my desk, unlock it, and call Tulsa. If she's not at the Mockingbird House, I'll have to go to her office. The last thing I need is for her to hear Judd was here and get a watered-down version.

"Hey, honey, this is a surprise," she answers on the second ring.

"I like that, butterfly, a lot. I'm heading out of the office. Where ya at?" I attempt to keep it light when all I want to do is run out the door, climb into my truck, and fly through town to get to her.

"Ledger, look at the time. I've already gone to the office, then to Mockingbird, hit the grocery store, and now I'm pulling up to the house." Fuck, the day completely got away from me. I look at my watch. It's nearing three.

"I guess I'm heading home. See you soon."

"Love you, drive safe," Tulsa replies.

"Love you, too. Always, butterfly." I hang up, walk out the door, make sure it's locked, and head to my truck. Getting to my woman is the only thing on my mind right now.

31

TULSA ROSE

"Honey, I'm home!" I feel like we only got off the phone five minutes ago when Ledger announces his presence. Surely, it's been longer than that, or time got away from me while I put away the groceries, three different types of pickles included I bought for the rest of the week, as well as steak, corn on the cob, and potatoes for dinner. I wasn't kidding about Ledger grilling tonight. The weather is still nice out for a Florida spring. Soon, it'll turn to summer, and we'll be escaping inside to get out of the heat.

"In the kitchen!" I'm just finishing my task, putting the canvas bags beneath the kitchen sink for the next time I head into town.

"This never gets old, butterfly, walking in the house, seeing you making it a home. Fuck, I'm a lucky damn man." He wraps his arms around my waist, lips gliding along my neck, whispering kisses along the skin as he moves up toward my ear.

"I'd say we're both lucky, wouldn't you think?" I turn

around. My hands slide up the outside of his muscular arms. They flex with every touch, straining his gray cotton shirt I'm on the tips of my toes, kissing the underside of his whiskered jaw.

"Fuck yeah, we are, which makes this ten times harder. You're all soft and sweet, in a good mood. I'm about to deliver news that's going to have you seeing red." He holds my lower back with one hand while the other cups the back of my head, dipping his knees to make it so we're at eye level.

"Well, if it's bad news, the least you can do is kiss me first." My stomach is in all kinds of knots, along with an unwelcome tremble that hits my nervous system.

"That I can do." He wedges a thick thigh of his between my own, backing me up against the kitchen counter. His teeth nip at my lower lip, tongue lapping at it to soothe the pain. My hands move to the back his head, nails digging in, as my mouth opens on a whimper. His tongue gains entrance and wraps around mine, and the worry I had disappears. When I'm with Ledger, it always does. It doesn't matter the place—the couch, the porch swing, in the truck, getting ready for work beside him—I know he'll always be my safe place to land.

"Christ, butterfly, the way you melt against me, it makes me lose my mind every damn time." His big work-roughened hands move to my hips, gripping them, making me wish I had the forethought to change out of my work clothes and into something that has fewer layers. He lifts me up and places me on top of the counter. "Beer?" he asks. I nod in response.

"Okay, time to fess up. It can't be that bad if beer is okay and you're not reaching for the liquor bottle," I tell his back.

The fridge light illuminates his body, the bottles clank, and he's popping off the tops, all before he responds.

"It's already taken care of. Or it will be, come this evening. Judd paid me a visit, breaking all kinds of protocol, but he knew not to approach you by yourself after the last time. It seems Ella is rearing her ugly-ass head, attempting to pin an assault charge." Ledger hands me my bottle and wedges himself between my now spread thighs, a hand on top of it, to hold me back when all I really want to do is get down, stomp my butt out of this house to kick ass and take names.

"Assault on you, I assume?" I ask, then take a healthy sip —okay, a gulp or two—from my bottle. Ledger does the same, emptying more than half. Maybe it's worse than what he led on.

"You'd think. She's trying to say you gave her a black eye on Saturday while you were at Hank's." The only thing I can do is laugh. Ella is reaching, far and wide. The sad thing is, I'm glad she's attacking me instead of Ledger. A claim like that against him could be career ending if it stuck. Which it won't. I'd have busted knuckles, while she'd try to attempt to pull my hair. Obviously, Ella plays dirty. "You're taking this better than I thought you would."

"There are three sides to every story—her side, my side, and the truth." I shrug my shoulders, not really worrying too much about it. "Besides, Judd went to you. I doubt it's serious, or I'd be making a statement." Nelle and Heather are going to get a massive kick out of this conversation, that's for sure.

"Hank took care of it, gave Judd the videos from the cameras in the bar. You're in the clear. Still pissed as fuck she'd pull this shit on you, when we all know she is pissed at me." Men are so dense, so I'm going to spell it out for him.

"Ledger, the more I look at the situation, the more certain I am she never wanted Montgomery. Or maybe she did, but when he dropped her, the stars in her eyes went to you. I mean, look at you. All you've accomplished, all her time and energy, it was all spent on you. In some warped way, Ella was hoping I'd never come back. I'm sure someone told her we were at Hank's. That grand display you made told everyone in town that Ledger Sinclair is officially off the market. Anyways, do I need to talk to Judd?" I finish my beer, no longer worried about the Ella situation.

"Damn, Tulsa Rose, you continue to amaze me. I'd be lying if I said I wasn't worried how you'd take the news."

"No one is running me out of town again, Ledger, least of all Ella." I put the beer back on the counter, since it's finished.

"You think I'd let you leave? That's not going to happen, not ever again. Now kiss your man. I've got dinner to cook and dessert to devour later." I lean into him and press my lips against his, feeling the hardness at my aching center. I swear for someone whose libido was practically non-exis-tent, he's made it to where I'm now a walking orgasm.

"I'm right where I belong, Ledger, here with you," I tell him. Another sweep of his lips against mine before he backs away.

"Damn straight. Now go make your call to Nelle." He grabs my phone from the other side of the counter, puts it in my hand, and then starts working in the kitchen.

"Oh, I am. And I'm calling your mom next. She's going to lose her mind." I look down at my phone, press the code because I'm too impatient for it to recognize my face, go to my call log, hit her name, then put the phone on speaker.

"This better be good, Tulsa Rose," Nelle answers the phone, breathless.

"Would I call you out of the blue knowing you're working if it wasn't?" My eyes bulge out of their sockets when I hear the slapping of skin and Chase's voice in the background telling her, "Hang up the phone, or you won't get my dick." Ledger is holding back a bark of laughter.

"Okay, this conversation is over. Love you, bye." I hit the end button repeatedly.

"I love my best friend, but there are some things no one should hear. Chase and she are clearly getting along, though." Ledger and I laugh together. Nelle deserves happiness. She's not allowed herself to be with anyone else since going through that fateful night in the emergency room, when I held her hand as the doctor told her she was losing her baby. After so much hurt and pain, I'm so incredibly happy to see her allowing herself to have something with Chase. Nelle might say I deserve everything, but so does she.

32

LEDGER

"**S**wing with me?" Tulsa asks when I step back on the front porch later in the evening after dinner was done and the dishes were taken care of. She made the dessert while I was preparing dinner—red velvet cupcakes with cream cheese frosting. They're currently in the fridge waiting for us to devour them later. Tulsa has her weird quirks about certain foods. Any type of chocolate cake or cupcakes have to be refrigerated, a cold glass of milk needs to be with it, and it has to be served in bed. I'd rather have her for dessert any day that ends in y, but she was adamant about baking, so I rolled with it.

I went back inside under the ruse of grabbing us a couple of more beers. I went after them first, set them on the counter, then took the stairs two at a time, hit the master bedroom, walk into the closet, and went to my safe. Keeping the jewelry pieces inside was a catch twenty-two, wondering if she'd need to go in there. Thankfully, she didn't. It's also where I keep both letters, Mont's and the one she wrote me that I've read more than a handful of times, stating how she was sorry, how she knew I was doing the right thing even when it hurt, and how she's loved me all along, even through the pain.

Montgomery was anal to the motherfucking tee, asking to keep her mom's wedding set, his dad's shot gun, and Mont's cross necklace his parents gave him, as well as a few of Tulsa's pieces that were priceless. The other stuff stayed at her house until she cleared it out. Now her jewelry box sits on the dresser, out in the open, her things are incorporated through the house, and I have no problem seeing a pair of shoes here, a bra there, a brush left on the bathroom counter. It makes this all the more real.

"You never have to ask," I tell her, placing the beers on the side table. She changed before baking the cookies, shucking the business casual look and giving me the Tulsa who loves tank tops and jean shorts. I stripped out of my boots and shirt, leaving me in just my jeans. Tomorrow is going to be hell, a long-as-fuck day since I spent all day in the office only to deal with Ella's aftermath.

I watch as she tucks her legs beneath her, sitting sideways, elbow on the back of the swing, hand in her hair holding it up in a bun. I take my place beside her. She moves into me. No matter how hot or cold it is, I'm bringing her body as close as possible to me. There's no nervousness running through my body. What I'm about to do is what I should have done seven years ago. Hell, I was already in Alabama, watching as she walked across that stage, accepting her diploma. Fuck, I made a lot of mistakes along the way. The right thing would have been to allow her the knowledge that I was there for her, cheering her on loud and proud, then meeting her off that stage and throwing her over my shoulder to bring her back home with me.

"Do you smell the orange blossoms tonight? I swear even though they're abandoned, I can still smell the citrus when the breeze blows just right." The sun is slowly setting, sinking behind the trees, making me love this land even more with the woman beside me.

"You always did love the orange trees. I can smell them, butterfly." I don't tell her they always reminded me of her when she was gone. I'd come out here, have a few beers, and think about what it'd be like to have her here beside me. "I'm not asking you to marry me, Tulsa Rose. I'm telling you we're getting married. The sooner, the better. I don't care about the logistics—in a courthouse, a church, inside or outside. All I care about at the end of the day is tying myself to you for all the years we have on this earth." I slip the ring off my pinky finger, take her hand in mine, and slide on her mother's ring, simple and dainty, so much like Tulsa. I knew this is what she would want.

"Oh God, Ledger, I love you." The hand that was holding her up drops to her mouth, covering it as tears roll down her cheeks. I bring her hand up to my mouth to softly kiss where I placed her ring before I move her until she's straddling my lap, hands cupping her face, attempting to swipe away the tears. But they keep coming. I can't keep up.

"I love you, Tulsa Rose. I did back then, I did while you were away, and I'll love you forever more."

"I, um, have news of my own. It might not be anything big. It could be a false alarm, but, well, I'm late." My eyes lower, and I breathe deeply. This is everything I've ever fucking wanted. Tulsa Rose in my arms, the possibility of our child in her belly. My hands grab her tank, pulling it up until the fabric is under her bare tits, nipples pebbling. There isn't any finesse when my fingers unsnap the buttons of her shorts, and I finally feast my eyes on what I was after.

"My baby could be inside you right now?" I palm her lower belly, relishing this moment.

"Yeah. I picked up one of those early response tests while I was at the grocery store. I'm going to take it in the morning." The look on my face when I focus on her mouth, watching as she tells me the real reason she went to the grocery store along with why she should wait, has her continuing, "The directions stated it would be best first thing in the morning." She shrugs her shoulders. There's no way either one of us will be sleeping tonight, not unless I take matters into my own hands.

"Then I guess the only way to make the time pass by quicker is to keep both of us busy." I stand up, needing to prove to her how much I love her in the form of getting inside my future wife. She wraps her legs around my waist, hands going to my shoulders. The beers are forgotten, and so is dessert. I'm about to show Tulsa what it means to be mine in every way imaginable.

EPILOGUE
TULSA ROSE

Two Years Later

"Are you ready to cut your cake?" I ask our son, William Montgomery Sinclair, named after Montgomery and my maiden name. Ledger's doing, stating that if we have a boy, he wants a piece of my brother with him always. This way, he did, and today, we're celebrating his first birthday. Heather and Hank are here, still refusing to acknowledge that there's something between them. They're ridiculous. Her car is either at his bar, or his is at Heather's. The cat is out of the bag. The only ones who need to catch up are them. Now, Nelle and Chase are another story entirely. They're rock solid, married for a year now, and she's got a slight waddle to her body as she carries my future niece or nephew. They want the gender to be a surprise, which is slowly eating me up inside. I want to buy all the cute things yet have to refrain. Beside them are

Chase's parents, visiting for the weekend, and Chase's brother, Mack, sits off to the side. The only one missing is Judd. I'm sure he'll stop by at one point or another. He handled the Ella situation. Went straight to her folks, which had them shocked with horror. They demanded she either straighten herself out or find a new place to live. She chose to leave town. It sucked for her parents, I'm sure. As for me, I celebrated right alongside with my girl tribe.

"Eyyy, Ma-ma!" He lifts his hands up for me to put him in his highchair, his booster seat we have set up on the pool deck. When I tell you I cried when he started pulling himself up on any surface and then proceeded to walk, I'm not exaggerating. I literally bawled. Ledger thought it was funny, which sent me into a tailspin. He pointed out that my hormones were a lot like when we first found out I was pregnant with William. The denial in thinking I wasn't pregnant was real. Nursing a baby has your hormones all jacked up, not to mention it's rare to get pregnant while nursing. The devious smile Ledger gave me once I calmed down from watching our son take his next step, literally and figuratively, should have told me everything, but damn. I've been tired even though I only work part-time. Heather watches William for me when she's not at her own part-time job at Sinclair roofing. I should have known my own body, though, especially considering William weened himself off the boob a month earlier. The sweet whispers from my husband when he was buried deep inside me, pumping my body full of his cum, telling me how he couldn't wait to see me pregnant again, to watch me nurse our child, and maybe this time, it would be a girl. Needless to say, it was Ledger this time who was prepared. A pregnancy test sat on the bathroom counter the next day, and the positive test was staring back at us. Two children under two. I'm not sure if this will be smart or unco-ordinated chaos. The plus is, this time around, I'm pregnant while my best friend is, too. She and Chase are currently expecting twins. And I got my wish. They purchased my childhood home from us last year, set down roots, only they eloped on a whim instead of having a wedding.

Mr. Flay worked his magic in helping with the donation front for The Women's Center. After I talked to Nelle, she brought up a good point and advised me to do this anony-mously. This small town of ours talks. One person would start a rumor about the reason I left when I was seventeen wasn't because of Mont's wishes; it'd be spun in a way in which I was pregnant, left town to have my baby and give it up for adoption. I rolled my eyes, but Nelle was right. I set up a corporation in my mom's maiden name. If someone did enough digging, they could figure out who helps them. Plus, as much as Nelle hurt from her past, she was trying to move on, not to forget but to forgive a piece of herself she didn't realize she was blaming. That left us with the other founda-tion I wanted to start, which is still in the early phases. Sad to say, unlike The Women's Center, where everything is set up and thriving, this new idea isn't, causing it to take twice as long. Soon, we'll get all the small items ironed out, but until then, it's a waiting game.

"Can I help?" Chase's niece, Sunny, walks up beside me in her princess crown, dress, gloves, and shoes.

"Of course. Will you keep William entertained while I grab the cake?" Everyone is in their seat, Heather and Hank on one side, Chase and Nelle on the other, the table in between. Ledger's seat is mysteriously empty.

"I will." Sunny's eyes light up, and while I usually wouldn't leave William or Sunny together on a pool deck with the fence down, I know the extra sets of eyes will watch them as well.

"I'll be right back," I tell the table. It's a hot day here in Orange Blossom. The breeze is non-existent, making the pool Ledger and I argued about non-stop perfect. I held my own. So much for him saying he only wanted a say in a few things. There was no way our home needed an ultra-modern square pool, with sharp angles and a three-tiered waterfall. Where I wasn't opposed to the waterfall, I added a small slide that everyone could use, with rocks carrying around it, blending the colors with the house. And I chose more of a kidney shape where deep end isn't twelve feet deep like Ledger originally wanted. That last part came directly from the pool company. Florida's water table would cause the pool to crack later down the road. No thanks. This damn pool was an investment enough, and then came the argument over the pool. How we were going to divide it. I got so pissed off that he wouldn't let me contribute half that I stormed out of the house, ran down the dirty driveway, across the road, and straight to the orange groves. The citrus scent calmed my frayed nerves, but I barely had a moment to myself before Ledger was there with me. He wouldn't compromise, and since I was seething mad, the only way to smooth things over between us was by him backing me up against the trunk of the tree behind me, dropping to his knees, lifting one thigh over his shoulder, sliding my thong beneath the sundress I was wearing to the side, and apologizing with his mouth, tracing *I am sorry* with the tip of his tongue. A different version when he's all about using numbers instead of letters. Needless to say, I gave in, and he paid for the pool after all.

"There you are." His arm bands around my back, pulling me in while holding William's smash cake with the other.

"Where else would I be?"

"We need to tell everyone. Today. Mom already noticed you bypassed the beer. Nelle will be onto you next." I roll my eyes. Neither of them would say a word, suspicious or not.

"Ledger Sinclair, I'm onto you. We'll tell them after William eats his cake." He wants to announce to the world that he can knock me up in little to no time at all, unbelievably proud of himself.

"That'll do. Thank you. Love you, butterfly." His lips peck mine.

"I love you." This is who my husband is, a man who has no problem staking his claim, any way he can.

EPILOGUE
LEDGER

Six Years Later

"Dad, is this where Uncle Mont is?" Our firstborn son, William Montgomery, asks. In my arms is our baby girl, Charlotte Marie, a mix of Tulsa's mom's name. We like to carry our loved ones' names through our children. James Oliver is currently with my wife, who's sitting on the bench nursing our baby boy. We quickly became a family of five over the last six years. If it were up to me, we'd have at least three more. Tulsa is good with the three we have now. That means it's up to me to convince her otherwise, which I have no doubt will be successful. Each of our children represents a loved one we lost along the way.

"Well, bud, he's with you wherever you go. This is where he's buried, though." It's a little hard for me to explain where my best friend currently is when in all fairness, he should be here with us, a wife and children of his own. Fuck, it's still hard every year when his birthday or the anniversary of his death comes around. Tulsa and I try our hardest to make the most of it, to celebrate him like he'd want, but there are those moments when we each go quiet, needing a minute to recover.

"And he was the greatest ever!" William exclaims. Charlotte reaches for my chin, demanding my attention.

"Yes, he was," I tell him, looking at our three-year-old little girl, who thankfully still likes to be held, given attention, and hasn't hit that mile-wide independent streak like her older brother. Each of our children are unique in their own way. William is independent and courageous, Charlotte is full of joy and love, and James is on the shy and timid side so far. Considering he's still a baby, it's hard to see his personality shine through.

"Da-da, we play?" Charlotte asks, hazel eyes like her mom and a smile that lights up a room.

"We have to ask mommy first." Taking the kids here isn't something we do a lot, but Tulsa Rose woke up this morning and said she needed it today. That's all it took. We ate breakfast, got the kids ready, then we were heading out the door. It wasn't any given moment, special date, or anything like that. Given that I wasn't going to let her do this alone, we all tagged along.

"Okay, I ask." Charlotte kicks her feet, asking to be put down. I drop to my haunches and let her go while holding my hand out for William. He takes it, and the three of us walk toward my wife, their mom, the glue that holds our family together. Here in Orange Blossom, the cemetery is small. The Williams occupy three plots, so it only made sense for me to put a concrete bench in their area for when

Tulsa or I visit. Which, truth be told, the day before I placed the ring on her finger, this is where you could find me, talking to Montgomery, telling him how much he was missed, that I got his letter and was ready to kick his ass if I could, and that I'd love Tulsa forever and eternity. He didn't give me a sign acknowledging my presence, though a breeze rippled the oak trees around the cemetery. I figure that was him doing his thing.

"Ma-ma, me play?" Charlotte holds her hands together in a praying gesture, a smile plastered across her face, giving off a cheesy grin.

"Sure. Do you want to go in the pool or to the park?" Tulsa asks her.

"Pool, pool, pool!" William jumps up and down, trying to overshadow what his sister wants. Knowing our luck, it's going to be the park. I'm with William on this. I'd rather we all go back home, hang around the pool, grill some burgers, and let the kids run free in the backyard. They've got a whole damn setup—tree fort, swing set, and trampoline.

"Pool!" Charlotte says excitedly. William and I got lucky today.

"Alright, we'll head home, get our suits on, lather on the sunscreen, and swim. Do you want to call Aunt Nelle and Uncle Chase to come over?" William nods his head vigorously. He's close in age with their son, Mason. Now Nelle is pregnant again, and given the Florida heat and humidity, the pool is the only place you'll find her.

"Pease and tanks," Charlotte says. Tulsa bends down to kiss her forehead. James detaches from her nipple, and I watch as my wife pulls her shirt down, looking at me while doing so. An impish grin is shot my way. Our sex life has yet to simmer down; we haven't hit that plateau. It doesn't matter the time of day, if we have a spare moment alone, we're shucking our clothes off, mouths fused to one another, and my cock is buried inside my wife, not leaving her tight warmth until she comes all over me.

"Alright, give me a few minutes," she tells the kids as she stands up, bringing James to her shoulder and walking toward me. "Will you give me a few minutes? I promise not to take long."

"You take all the time you need. I'll take James and settle the kids in the car. We'll be alright. We dodged a bullet. Three kids in a park on a busy Saturday? Woman, you are a saint," I whisper so Charlotte doesn't hear and change her mind. "And, butterfly?"

"Yeah, Ledger," she responds breathlessly.

"Don't think I didn't see what you did there. The kids go down for a nap or bedtime, whichever comes first, you're mine." A promise I'll be keeping. She transfers James to me but doesn't say a word. Her eyes lids flutter closed, and she takes a deep breath, attempting to compose herself, and then steps away.

"Come on, William, Charlotte, let's load up. Mom needs a minute with your grams, gramps, and uncle," I tell the kids. Tulsa always asks if I want to stop and visit my father. We probably would if he weren't hundreds of miles away, buried in a national cemetery. A place plots, headstones, and the likes may be where their final resting place is, but I'm a firm believer that your loved ones are aways surrounding you.

"Race you, Char!" The kids run ahead of me, twenty or so feet, staying on the grass, stopping when they get to the massive SUV we now need with three kids. I make quick work of opening the back door. The older two climb in,

William in the third row, Charlotte behind the driver's seat in the second row.

"Buckle up. I'll check on you two once I get James loaded, alright?" I set James in his infant carrier behind the passenger seat and clasp his harness, making sure it's tight without being too tight, and because my body calls to Tulsa's whenever she's near, I turn around. She's walking toward us, a soft serene smile on her face, the swish of her sundress bouncing around her thighs, and damn if it doesn't solidify that she and our kids are fucking everything to me. Montgomery was right. There's only one man on this earth who could love her the way I do, and I'm the lucky bastard who gets to spend the rest of my life with her.

Want more Men in Charge? Secret Obsession, an Age Gap, Small Town Romance is coming June 11!

Amazon

Prologue

Twelve Years Earlier

Trace

"Dad, we're here," Wes yells through the house, nineteen damn years old and still hollering through the house as he makes his way inside. It's been the two of us since he was discharged from the hospital. Sure, I had help from my parents. We even lived with them until Wes was five or six years old, then it was time to get my shit together, work less than sixty hours a week, and allowing daycare and my mom to raise Wes. I found a rental near town, in a good school zone, and we started our life without being under my parents roof. There was a shit ton of *oh fucks* along the way, burnt dinner, Wes staying up too late because I was working late, wanting to spend time with him, laundry piling up, and all the other stuff that comes with being a single father. A learning curve to say the least, we managed it after quite a few trial and errors, half the time I felt like I was failing him, then my dad would reel my ass in, lay out on the line, and tell me to quit feeling sorry for myself. If I were failing, I would have given Wes up for adoption when Misty willingly walked out of his life. I didn't blame her, how could I, she was only a year older than me, a one night stand, in another town, broken condom, and six weeks later Misty found me on a jobsite to give me the news. There wasn't a doubt in my mind when she said her options, adoption or abortion. I quickly gave her the option to pay for medical bills, make sure she had a place to live while pregnant, and I'd take our child. So, at the age of nineteen, newly graduated from high school, I worked like a dog to give her life she deserved while growing Wes inside her belly. The minute he was born, she signed over her parental rights, asking me to take him away, and then left the hospital against medical advice. No one ever saw her again, sucks that she willingly missed out on all the good that could have been in her life.

"In the kitchen, bud," I reply, a beer in my hand, raised to my mouth taking a long as fuck pull, downing half the bottles contents. I'm feeling every bit of my thirty-six years old after work today, the hours are long, and the sun is hotter. Especially when your job involves framing houses on the side, I dabble in my own version of working with my hands, building kitchen cabinets. I look around at our home, a small three-bedroom, one bathroom house, built in the 1940's, we moved in here once Wes hit his teenager years and I've been working on it ever since. I finish the rest of my beer when my son and his girlfriend round the corner, a damn good thing too, I'm unprepared for the girl he's brought home.

"Hey dad, Josie, this is my dad, Trace, dad, this is my girl-friend Josie," I lower my bottle of beer, as my boy hits me with a hug, pulling him in with one arm, eyes locking his girls, her vivid blue eyes, blonde hair, and full lips are locked on mine.

"Nice to meet you Josie," Wes and I pull back from our hug, the bottle of beer is placed on the new counter tops there were just installed this past week, unlike myself Wes went to college a few hours south, his first year, only coming home for the holidays and now spring break, this time bringing home his girlfriend.

"Nice to meet you too, Mr. Gaines," she uses my last name, as our hands meet one another's in a handshake. Fuck me, God damn it, this is not what I want, the dumb flesh between my thighs, attempts to make its presence known, this is not the time or the place for a hard on, especially for the beauty in front of me, she's young, too young, half my age, my sons girlfriend, tell that to my cock which is currently twitching in my jeans, her eyes lingering on my body doesn't fucking help. She's forbidden fruit and damn if I don't want a taste.

"Please call me Trace, Mr. Gaines is my father," the dryness in my throat from thoughts of Josie make me realize

I need another drink. Shit, my father is a fuck of a lot older than I am, another difference between my parents and myself. Where I'm blissfully unwedded, they were married, went and saw the world for five or so years before having me, settling down in our small town here in Tennessee, planting roots, and never moving out of my childhood home until Wes and myself got our own place. Then they built a home, one that isn't as big, more manageable, allowing them to come and go as they please on their jaunts to hit the next casino.

"Alright, Trace," Wes already has his head in the fridge, pulling out a beer for himself when Josie our hands finally disengage.

"If you're drinking, you're not driving. I'm taking a shower, there ain't shit in the fridge yet, we'll go out to Cooper's for dinner. Tomorrow I'll pick up groceries," seeing as how he and his girlfriend got into town on a Friday afternoon, the only reason I'm home now my foreman didn't get the permits pulled from city hall last week for a job that starts next week.

"Thanks, it's been a while since we've been to Cooper's, how's Cooper and his wife doing?" Wes may not have been there for a while, I make it a point to see my friend and his wife at least once a week, whether it's to have a beer with a steak for dinner or I'm over at his house while his wife, Gia whips up a dinner.

"They're good, you'll see them tonight for yourself," I tip my head at Josie, open the fridge, grab another beer, hoping it'll help calm my dick down, and if not, I'll use my hand to get myself under control. "Get yourselves settled, I'll be out in a few," I clap Wes's back and head toward the bathroom, popping.

Josie

"What did you say?" I ask Wes, my eyes moving away from his father Trace, watching him walk out of the kitchen. The man can fill out a pair of jeans, white cotton shirt stretched along his upper body, tapered waist, and long legs with a slow easy gait.

"I'm going to go grab our bags, make yourself comfortable," the guy I've been dating for the past few months tells me now that I'm knocked out of my revere of salivating over his father. God, I hope there's no visible sign of drool because my mouth is most definitely watering.

"Do you want any help?" Not for the first time am I having second thoughts about coming home with Wes. He's a good looking guy, more on the lean side than Trace, boyish in appearance whereas his dad is one thousand percent all rugged man, obviously these thoughts weren't in mine up until a few moments ago. It was on the four hour ride in Wes's car that had me thinking, heading home would have been smarter, working the full week back at my parents realty office, earn some money, and then head back to college once break was over.

"Nah, I got it. Take a look around, this won't take me long," Wes's hand meets mine, squeezes my fingers once, drops them, and lets out a loud belch, blasting the room with its echo. I roll my eyes, never in my life will I understand why college boys feel the need to showcase their lack of manners, laughing it off, unlike when Trace left, I don't watch as Jace walks toward the door. I blow out a puff air, wondering again how I got myself into this situation, then do as Wes suggests, when we pulled in the driveway of Wes and

Trace's place, the outside was well manicured, green grass, lawn mower tracks running horizontally in a pattern showing it was cut in the past day or so, hedges beneath the windows along the front of the house. Wes parked beside what I assume is Trace's truck, we walked through the door, dark walls, wood floors, and unobstructed views clear to the back of the house. Now, I'm left to my own devices, meandering out of the kitchen and into the living room, the dark walls continue through the house, making it dark and moody, a place where you can enjoy a cup of coffee in the early morning as the sunrises or relax in the evenings, a blanket on your lap with the fireplace putting off heat to lull you into the best sleep ever.

I walk towards the hallway, wondering if I'm sleeping in Wes's bedroom or my own, unsure of how these things work, seeing as how this is my first time doing this sort of thing. Each door I've come across is closed, only confusing me further. Maybe I should have stayed in the kitchen instead of allowing myself to wander around.

"Josie," my name is drawn out as the door in front of my opens with a sharpness as if the occupant inside is in a hurry. I'm completely unprepared for the view I'm presented, if I wasn't drooling before I certainly am now. My eyes zero in on the rivulet of water that slowly moves from his muscular pec, dragging down inch by inch, hitting a solid wall of abs, one slope giving way to another slope, I count each, one, two, three, four, the crips white towel keeping it from going further and I'm cursing myself. I should not be licking my lips, my imagination should not be running away from itself, and I most assuredly should not be staring at my boyfriend's father.

"Fuck it," comes from Trace, one minute I'm standing in

front of him, lost in the way he looks, wondering how he would feel against me when I'm literally pulled inside the room Trace was leaving, door slamming behind with the hand that isn't wrapped around my waist.

"Trace," I pant, as sure as my footsteps were to follow him, they have no problem going backwards, Trace crowding me in as my back meets the wood door, the two of us in the bathroom, the fog swirling around us from his shower, his dark hair is wet, the only thing he has on is the towel.

"One taste," his hand leaves my wrist, cupping my cheek, thumb pulling on my lower lip, a whimper escapes me, "Shit, that mouth, I need it, and I'm gonna take it," Trace states, I must nod my head in the answer he was waiting for, his other hand trails my outer thigh, the short flowy skirt is no match for Trace's work roughened hands, skating a path higher and higher, his head dips down, caging me in with his body, the skirt I'm wearing is not match for his worked roughened hands, slide higher and higher. My eyes close and Trace makes his move, the quiet of the house, Wes probably steps away from returning in the house, and I'm at war with myself. I'm not this person, this isn't who I am, those are my last thoughts as Trace's mouth meets mine, unprepared for the feeling, one sweep of his lips does me in. The thought of kissing my boyfriend's father and how wrong it is, flies out the window. In its place is how this feels, the nipping of my lower lip, Trace licking at it to soothe the slight pain away, and when he pushes deeper, his tongue sliding inside, kissing me like I've never been kissed before, my own hands kneading his sides, and feeling his thick length pressed against my lower abdomen. Trace's fingers tighten along my upper thigh, his thumb sweeping dangerously closer to the edge of my lace panties, dragging the digit lower in doing so, my body weakens, thankful for the door and Trace's firm body to hold me up.

"Yo, dad, Jo!" All good things must come to an end, and Wes's voice breaks apart our kiss, so fast, I'm no longer holding onto Trace, now I'm pushing him away.

"Oh my God, what have we done, this was a mistake," I clamor to get away from Wes's father, there's no way I'll ever be able to look at him again and not think of this very moment or the fact that I've done the one thing I promised myself I'd never do. I cheated on my boyfriend with his father.

Amazon

ABOUT THE AUTHOR

Tory Baker is a mom and dog mom, living on the coast of sunny Florida where she enjoys the sun, sand, and water anytime she can. Most of the time you can find her outside with her laptop, soaking up the rays while writing about Alpha men, sassy heroines, and always with a guaranteed happily ever after.

Sign up to receive her **Newsletter** for all the latest news!

Tory Baker's Readers is where you see and hear all of the news first!

[f] [o] [BB] [g] [d]

ACKNOWLEDGMENTS

This is about to get very long and very wordy because that's just who I am. I've got so many people to thank and shout out that I hope no one is forgotten. When I set out about change this year, I was all freaking in. I'm extremely fortunate you all are taking this wild ride with me. The depth in these stories it fills my heart up with a joy I lost along the way and my cup couldn't runneth over without your support!

NaShara McClaeb: ya'll can thank her for that gym scene, sending me a reel on instagram telling me I need this in a book but with my twist. There have been many a conversations we've had about this story. Every time I struggled, she was there to kick my ass into gear. I can't thank you enough! Also, we're hitting up a hockey game in Tampa this year.

To my kids: A & A without you I'd be a shell of myself. You helped me find myself in a moment of darkness. Thank you for picking up the slack around the house while I was knee deep in this deadline, cooking, cleaning, and taking care of Remi (our big lug of a Weimaraner). I love you to infinity times infinity.

Jordan: Oh my lanta, the hand holding, the me calling you hysterically crying or laughing, day or night, good or bad. I love you bigger than outer space. If it weren't for you pushing me to write, to see the potential in me, I wouldn't be here.

Mayra: My sprinting partner extraordinaire. Girlfriend, we made it through 2022 ahead of schedule. One day I will fly my butt to California to hug you!

Julia: How do you deal with me and my extra sprinkling of commas? The real MVP, the one who deals with my scatter-brained self, missing deadlines, rescheduling like crazy, and the person I live vicariously through social media.

Amie Vermaas Jones: Thank you for always and I do mean always helping me on my last minute shit. It never fails that I'm sending you an SOS asking for your eyes. Beach days are happening and SOON!

Thank you for being here, reading, not just my books but any Author's stories. We do appreciate you more than you know, the reason why we can live out our dream is for readers, bloggers, bookstagrammers, bookmakers, Authors, and everyone in between. THANK YOU!

All this to say, I am and will always be forever grateful, love you all!

ALSO BY TORY BAKER

Men in Charge

Make Her Mine

Staking His Claim

Billionaire Playboys

Playing Dirty

Playing with Fire

Playing With Her

Vegas After Dark Series

All Night Long

Late Night Caller

One More Night

About Last Night

One Night Stand

Hart of Stone Family

Tease Me

Hold Me

Kiss Me

Please Me

Touch Me

Feel Me

Diamondback MC Second Gen.

Obsessive

Seductive

Addictive

Protective

Deceptive

Diamondback MC

Dirty

Wild

Bare

Wet

Filthy

Sinful

Wicked

Thick

Bad Boys of Texas

Harder

Bigger

Deeper

Hotter

Faster

Hot Shot Series

Fox

Cruz

Jax

Saint

Getting Dirty Series

Serviced (Book 1)

Primed (Book 2)

Licked (Book 3)

Hammered (Book 4)

Nighthawk Security

Never Letting Go (Easton and Cam's story)

Claiming Her (Book 1)

Craving More (Book 2)

Sticky Situations (Travis and Raelynn's story)

Needing Him (Book 3)

Only His (Book 4)

Carter Brothers Series

Just One Kiss

Just One Touch

Just One Promise

Finding Love Series

A Love Like Ours

A Love To Cherish

A Love That Lasts

Stand Alone Titles

Nailed

Going All In

What He Wants

Accidental Daddy

Love Me Forever

Gettin' Lucky

It's Her Love

Meant To Be

Breaking His Rules

Can't Walk Away

Carried Away

In Love With My Best Friend

Must Be Love

Sweet As Candy

Falling For Her

All Yours

Sweet Nothings Book 3—Tory Baker

Loving The Mountain Man

Crazy For You

Trick— The Kelly Brothers

Friend Zoned

His Snow Angel

223 True Love Ln.

Hard Ride

Slow Grind

1102 Sugar Rd.

The Christmas Virgin

Taking Control

Unwrapping His Present

Tempting the Judge